Gangsters
Wives

Gangsters
Wives

LEE MARTIN

NO EXIT PRESS

First published in 2007 by No Exit Press
P.O.Box 394, Harpenden, Herts, AL5 1XJ
www.noexit.co.uk

A CIP catalogue record for this book is available from the British
Library.

ISBN 10: 1 84243 222 2 (Hardcover)
ISBN 13: 978 1 84243 222 8 (Hardcover)
ISBN 10: 1 84243 223 0 (Royal Paperback)
ISBN 13: 978 1 84243 223 5 (Royal Paperback)

For Des McKeogh
1943–2006
Sadly Missed

Gangsters
Wives

1

———⟫⟨———

Sadie Ross was at it that morning. Lately it seemed she was always at it. Young men mostly. With good bodies and stamina. The pool boy, a waiter from the bistro where she lunched with her girlfriends, her hairdresser (who surprisingly wasn't gay), her personal trainer from one of the gyms she frequented to keep her fit body even fitter, and that day, Tony, the boy who did odd jobs around the house. She wasn't that fussy really. As long as they didn't talk too much and wore a condom, and of course gave her satisfaction, almost anyone would do. If it crossed her mind it could get depressing. So she rarely allowed it to. Bollocks to it. But toy boys, who would've thought it? Not that Sadie was old. Thirty-five was nothing these days she knew. Thirty-five, and pretty damn good for her age. Tall and blonde. Natural, with just a little help from the bottle. Blonde down below too. Matching collar and cuffs, her husband Eddie called it. Brazilian of course. Figure still firm, and face unlined. Besides, in the twenty-first century anything was possible if you had the cash. And she and Eddie did. Nips, tucks, boob jobs, liposuction. She'd still look good into her fifties and beyond. Only sometimes she saw Eddie looking at her, and she wondered what he was thinking. Mates of his had dumped their first wives and moved down a generation, or even two, for another go with young birds who were nowhere near close to thinking about plastic surgery. But that thought depressed her too, so she left it alone as well.

So that morning, the only odd job Tony was doing was servicing the lady of the house.

Christ, if Eddie knew, she thought, as Tony threw her down on top of her marital bed. There'd be murders done. Literally. Eddie Ross wasn't a man to be trifled with. The polite term for how he earned his living was businessman/entrepreneur. In fact he was a gangster. A thief. An armed robber when necessary, and a torturer if that was what was needed. He was the brains behind a loose conglomerate of men who worked together when a job came up. Eddie planned the work, and they did as they were told. In fact if Eddie had put as much effort into some kind of legitimate business, he'd probably have been a captain of industry. But Eddie hated anything legit. Anything straight. 'No fun,' he'd say. 'No fucking fun at all.' So Eddie kept his eyes and ears open for a spot of anything that brought in fast, clean cash, and everyone was happy. But in that kind of business, things could change fast.

* * *

Eddie Ross had been at it too that morning. A nice little tickle which had yielded about forty grand in cash as his share. A hit on a diamond wholesaler on the south coast swiftly turned into real money at a fence in Guildford. Used notes, mainly tens and twenties, with a few fifties thrown in, which he didn't like. People were too suspicious of fifties these days. Didn't like taking them. Too many snides about. But money was money. So he reckoned he'd give them to his coke dealer for a pile of charlie and let him get the grief of getting rid of them. Eddie grinned to himself as he gunned the engine of his dark blue Audi A8 off the motorway. He was proud of his motor, which he'd got brand new. It looked like a doctor's car but went like shit off a shovel, and he dropped a gear and put his foot down as he headed for home. Everything had gone so sweet that he was early. Give Sadie a surprise was his plan. A quick fuck, then a long lunch at their favourite Thai restaurant in Greenwich. It would be a nice change to have a shag with his missus, instead of some mystery he'd pulled on a night out with the lads. A real nice change. Not that he didn't know that she played away. Course he did. He wouldn't have been Eddie Ross otherwise. Silly cow thought she'd got one over him. More than one. Lots more. But Eddie really didn't care. The bloom was well and truly off the rose with Sadie. Not that she didn't keep herself tidy, because she did. Always on a diet. Always exercising. And when they went out together, which Eddie had to admit wasn't as often as it used to be, she took great care with her appearance, and had lot of other blokes frothing at the mouth. But Eddie was just a bit tired of her. And there were always ways and means to get a bit of revenge. But that could wait until the time was right.

Eddie grinned again and looked in the rear view mirror at his reflection. Not bad for a man in his early forties, he thought. He was big, and well in shape thanks to his personal trainer at the gym. He knew the young bloke was shafting Sadie, and he would've been tied to his Nautilus machine with so many weights loaded on it his arms would rip out of their sockets if Eddie had cared more. His time would come too. Eddie knew some very nasty boys, who'd be happy to do him a favour for old time's sake. Best served cold, his dad had always said. Revenge. Best served cold. As the car shot past an articulated lorry Eddie stroked his bald, bullet head and grinned some more. There was just one cloud over Eddie's parade. Later that month he was up at the Bailey on robbery and conspiracy charges. A bit of bad luck after a mail van robbery on the old Great West Road had led to Eddie being given a pull and charged. Fucking bent coppers, thought Eddie as his smile vanished. Can't trust the bastards, that's the trouble. And straight ones were even worse. You never knew where you were with them. His number one inside man in the Met had gone and been done for conspiracy to pervert, had offered Eddie up as a sweetener to lessen the charge, and it was unfortunate timing that Eddie hadn't got rid of the incriminating evidence at the lockup in Custom House that he used as a bolt-hole. He'd always thought no one knew about the place, but the slag of a copper must've been a better detective than Eddie thought he was, and one morning at six there'd been warrants served at the house and the garage, and Eddie had been caught bang to rights. Of course there were ways and means there too, which was why Eddie had been at work the previous couple of days. Money talks, he thought as he left the motorway, and the money from the diamond robbery had a lot of talking to do if he was going to walk free from court.

Eddie slowed as he drove through the A and B roads that led to the house just outside Laindon in Essex. It was an ugly bastard of a place. A mish-mash of Art Deco and fake Tudor, but Eddie didn't care. As long as it had a snooker room, an inside swimming pool and a home cinema it was all right with him. And it had all of those and more. After all, he didn't have to look at it when he was inside. He steered the car into the private road where the house sat and pushed the control on the dash to open the double gates, and he was home and dry. Job done.

Sadie was just reaching the point of orgasm when she heard the rumble of her husband's motor hitting the drive. You couldn't mistake the unique sound of the V8 engine as it pulled through the gates.

'Shit,' she shouted as Tony hit the short strokes. 'It's Eddie.'

Tony flinched and tried to withdraw out of her, but she sank her acrylic nails into his shoulders and pulled him in deeper.

'Keep going,' she said through gritted teeth. 'I want to come, you little fucker.'

But Tony had lost it and she felt him shrink, pull out and roll over, the Durex slipping off his cock.

He was pasty white with fright as he struggled into his T-shirt and jeans and headed for the door. He knew Eddie and his reputation, and he wasn't about to stick around and get his legs broken. It had been crazy to get involved with Sadie in the first place, but she was something else in bed. And generous with it. 'Not that way stupid,' said Sadie. 'Use the sodding window.'

The bedroom was on the first floor with a balcony outside the French doors leading to a narrow balcony overlooking the back garden, and Tony did as he was told. Better a broken leg from a fall than two from Eddie. 'What about these?' said Sadie as she tossed him his underwear. Calvin Kleins. Real ones. Twenty quid a pair from a boutique in Lakeside, not cheap knockoffs from a stall in Romford market. Tony grabbed them, hopped over the balcony and landed on a flower bed just as Eddie opened the front door.

He headed straight upstairs to find his wife straightening the bedspread, dressed in a silk kimono. 'What are you doing here?' she said. 'I wasn't expecting you 'til tonight.'

'All done and dealt with darlin'.' he replied. 'And look at what I've got.'

He upended the sports bag he was carrying and

loose notes fell onto the bed like leaves in a storm. 'Christ,' said Sadie. 'A result.'

'Oh yes.'

'How much?'

'Forty K, give or take. Not bad for a night or two's work.'

'You can say that again. Shopping?' Next to fucking her boys, and lunching with her mates, shopping was Sadie's favourite pastime.

'That can wait,' he said as he stuck his hand under her wrap and slid his fingers inside her. 'You're all wet,' he said. 'What have you been up to?'

Sadie almost pissed herself with fear. If Eddie knew what she had been doing... 'It's you doll,' she replied. 'And all that dough. It's enough to make a nun wet.'

'And you ain't no nun,' said Eddie. 'How about a quickie, then lunch? You can shop tomorrow.'

Sadie forced a smile. Quickies with Eddie were the reason that she used her boys. 'Lovely darlin'.' she said. 'Can't think of anything nicer.'

So, on a bed of money Sadie was shagged for the second time that day, and it wasn't even lunchtime yet. But she knew it wouldn't last long. Eddie's fucks never did. And for that she was grateful.

2

Connie Smith, Eddie's partner in the robbery on the diamond merchant, got home at roughly the same time as Eddie. But it was a different kind of homecoming, and a very different location. Not for him a mansion in Essex, but a little end-of-terrace house on the Isle of Dogs where he'd lived with his parents all his life, and had inherited when they'd both died within months of each other ten years before. True, he'd added a conservatory at the back and a brand new kitchen, but Connie had always been careful with his money, and didn't like to be too flash. He'd seen an awful lot of his mates go potty with a few quid, down the casinos and at Walthamstow Dogs in their Bentleys and Jags after a good result, and end up behind bars when someone took exception and grassed them up. Connie drove a Ford Mondeo and liked it. He also knew he didn't have to work for a bit with the forty grand he had in a sports bag, identical to Eddie's. Good graft. He worried about Eddie too. He was a flash monkey, and up in front of a jury at the end of the month for a job that Connie had helped out with. Connie and Joseph and Robbo. They'd been working together since they were kids in the Seventies. Little stuff at first, but as the Eighties came and went they'd moved up into the big time. Armed robbery was their game of preference, and they were bloody good at it. But they were up for any bit of business worth a few bob. They lived charmed lives with the help of backhanders here, there and everywhere. Substantial backhanders, and if they didn't work, a little ultra violence usually did the trick. And Connie was always up for that. True, there'd been a few pulls now and then, with maybe a month or two on remand. But never a guilty verdict. Eddie had got nicked a few months before because of a copper on the payroll who decided to turn Queens to save his own arse. But not a word had been spoken. Eddie had remained staunch. Followed the code. No grassing. Anyway, Eddie had a terrific brief, even if he did cost an arm and a leg, so he wasn't inside long.

Everyone knew Connie was the maddest fucker of them all when it came to putting the frighteners on. Which was exactly why, when the tickle down on the coast had come up, Eddie had rowed Connie in. Joe and Robbo had moaned a bit, but it was strictly a two man operation and both Eddie and Connie had agreed to drop the other two a few bob to keep them sweet.

Connie parked his motor in the resident's zone, took the sports bag, and went to see his wife Niki.

Now, Connie had never had much luck with women. Not until Niki came along. He didn't have the patter that the others did. Didn't have the chat, or the looks. His thinning red hair (that he'd started to lose when in his early twenties) didn't help either. He'd always hated being called a ginger. Hated the nicknames it earned him, which was one reason he'd turned into such a vicious bastard. But then he'd hated going bald worse. No bird ever looked at him twice after that started happening. So one day he'd gone on the net and started surfing. That was when he found a site where young Russian women advertised themselves as looking for husbands in the West. Connie couldn't believe his luck when he found Niki's photo and sparse details. She'd been born twenty years previously in a village outside Moscow. Orphaned at eleven, she'd lived with her grandmother and grandfather until their death and now she wanted out. She was beautiful, olive skinned with green eyes and long, thick black hair. Surely no woman who looked like that could be interested in him, but she was.

Connie plucked up courage to reply to the advertisement, and after a brief courtship by e-mail he'd sent her a ticket and she came over on holiday. He'd heard of women using false photographs to interest men, and as he stood waiting at the arrivals barrier at Heathrow he wondered if she could be as perfect as she appeared to be on the screen of his PC, but she was. More so in the flesh. Within a month they were married, despite the piss-taking from the rest of the gang. And now she was Mrs Niki Smith. Left alone regularly as she was, she spent the time practising her English skills. In Russia, her family had been the proud owners of a satellite box and dish, which was where Niki had learnt most of her English idiom. Now she loved *EastEnders*, although it seemed to have little to do with the East End that she lived in. But she gobbled up the slang and used it as much as possible, much to the amusement of Connie and his crowd. But she didn't care.

Niki was waiting in the living room when Connie let himself in. He noted that the place was spotlessly clean, just like he expected it. Niki was an extremely good housekeeper, and that was where Connie liked her to be. In the house. Although she could drive he didn't allow her a licence, or the use of his car. She had no bank account or credit card. He doled out cash when she needed it. Sparingly. He took her shopping and bought her what she needed or wanted. Louis Vuitton handbags, Chanel make-up, anything. She was his exotic bird in a gilded cage. She rarely left the house alone, just occasionally to have lunch with Sadie and the wives of the other members of the gang. Gangsters' wives. Women he could trust. Or so he thought.

He was also insanely jealous of any other man looking at her. A couple of times when they'd been out together he'd seen a young bloke giving her the once over, so he'd taken them outside and delivered a good kicking. In fact, sometimes he thought that was the best part of the marriage.

So Niki knew her place, but Connie never noticed the looks she gave him when his back was turned. Her father and his forefathers before him had been Cossacks. Men who were even more frightening in their capacity for violence than Connie and his gang. She was her father's daughter. Niki wanted what the West could provide. She'd married Connie to get it all, and all she had was a well-decorated prison in East

London. When she lay next to him in their bed at night, she often cried herself to sleep. But they were tears of rage, not sorrow. As he mounted her for his twice weekly orgasm, which gave her no pleasure, she knew that one day she would have to kill him to escape. How she envied Sadie, and Joseph and Robbo's wives, their perfect lives nothing like hers. Except nothing in this world is perfect, as they'd all discovered one way or another.

3

Kate Ellis for instance. Beautiful Kate. She of the long red hair and porcelain skin. Married to Robbo Ellis and daughter of Johnny Wade, one of East London's most feared villains of the latter half of the twentieth century. The good old days when anything went, on the dirty streets of Plaistow, Beckton and Canning Town, where Johnny made his fortune from protection and drugs, prostitution and money laundering, and where more than one chancer, trying to muscle in on Johnny's territory, found himself trussed up in the boot of a stolen motor and sent to a watery grave in the old docks.

Johnny was an old man now, but still had the kind of respect in the area that only fear can bring.

Robbo had worshipped him, but Kate hated him. He had ruled his extended family with the same kind of violence as he ruled his manor. Four sons who'd accepted anything the old man doled out. Then Kate came along. A late child when her mother and father were already middle-aged. He tried the same medicine with her. Kate had lost count of the times he'd taken his belt to her when she was a teenager, only interested in clothes and house music. So when handsome Robbo Ellis had come along, all flowers, chocolates, flash motors, expensive restaurants and clubbing up West, how could she resist? The answer was she hadn't. She gave up her closely guarded virginity in the bedroom of his flat in Limehouse one Saturday night and he was everything she'd dreamed of, passionate yet tender. Robbo proposed on a floating Chinese restaurant on Millwall Harbour next to Docklands Arena a few months later, where they'd seen Oasis play from the VIP area, and Liam Gallagher had smiled at Kate over chow mein after the concert, as the band dined at the next table. There were roses and an engagement ring worth fifty-grand, with a diamond as big as an egg. So how could she refuse? Once again she couldn't, and the waiter brought champagne as the entire staff and clientele cheered at the news of her acceptance.

Kate was nineteen at the time.

The wedding was one of the biggest the area had ever seen. White Rollers ferried the family and guests to the Wren Church in Poplar, then a glass carriage pulled by four white horses took the bride and groom to the wedding breakfast in a five star hotel just opened at Canary Wharf. Enough Cristal champagne was drunk to sink the Titanic and Kate was glowing in a couture wedding dress that she'd seen in *Vogue*. The wedding pictures wouldn't have looked out of place in the pages of a glossy magazine—if the whole thing hadn't been funded by violence, extortion and drug money.

Kate had never been so happy, but that was all about to change.

Robbo quickly turned from the loving fiancee to an abusive husband. On their wedding night at the hotel he beat Kate black and blue when she refused his drunken advances. This was after leaving her alone for hours in the bridal suite as he drank whiskey with his mates in the bar, until dawn broke and the last of the guests made their drunken way home. But Robbo was no fool. He didn't hit her where it showed. Not her face. Just her body, so that on their honeymoon in St Lucia, Kate could not wear the bikinis she had so happily bought as part of her trousseau, but instead had to do with a mumsy one-piece bathing-suit purchased from the hotel boutique. 'You tell your father what I've done,' said Robbo, 'and I'll kill you.'

But Johnny wouldn't have cared. 'No more than you deserve,' he would have said. Kate knew, because she'd witnessed the damage her father had done to her mother, Dolly, over the years. Black eyes, split lips, and even the occasional broken bone. That was Johnny's way, and Kate had pleaded with her mother a hundred times to leave her brutal husband, but her mother had been too frightened to go. 'He'd find me darlin',' said her mum. 'Hunt me down and kill me. I belong to him, see. Body and soul.'

Then kill him first, Kate thought, but she never said a word.

When the cancer hit Dolly Wade it was almost a relief. She lived for just a few months more, long enough to see her daughter engaged, but not long enough to attend the wedding, or witness what happened afterwards.

It seemed to Kate that Johnny hardly noticed his wife's absence. Only moaning about his lack of tea in bed in the morning, and a bit of the other after Sunday dinner.

You disgust me, thought Kate as her brothers laughed at his joke. Within a few months of Kate's nuptials he'd met and moved a younger woman into the family home. A brassy blonde he'd picked up at one of the nightclubs he still had control over in Ilford. After that Kate hardly saw him.

Not that she cared. She'd gone from one abusive relationship to another, and it seemed to her that was exactly what she deserved.

So now, she and Robbo lived in splendour in a detached house in Harold Hill. Robbo, Joseph, Eddie and Connie carried out their various crimes, and Kate took her regular beatings stoically. But Robbo was getting worse. More violent as he grew older, and now sometimes Kate had to layer on the concealer and wear dark glasses to hide the marks from her husband's fists when she went to the shops, or to meet her friends.

Sadie was the closest to her, and they met for long lunches when the men were away, as they often were. 'Leave the fucker Katie,' she said.

But Kate knew, as her mother knew before her, that it would do no good. 'He'd find me Sade,' she'd say, mimicking Dolly's words. 'Hunt me down and kill me.'

'Bastard,' said Sadie. But she knew it was true. The men they'd married treated their wives as property. Bought and paid for. And woe betide any of them who got out of line. Sadie knew that she was playing with fire when she played away from home. But she had long ago stopped considering the consequences.

4

Then there was lovely little Poppy. Just a shade over five foot tall, with coffee coloured skin from her mixed-race parents. Father a rudeboy from Jamaica, long time ago gone into the dark midnight, mother a reconstructed mod who got knocked up one night after a Bad Manners gig at the 101 Club in Clapham Junction. Mum and daughter lived together in a council flat in Bethnal Green. Poppy didn't guard *her* virginity at all. She gave it up one afternoon when she was thirteen to a slightly older boy, down where the rubbish was kept under the flats. Even now when she has sex she could still catch a whiff of the rotten garbage overflowing from the bins. They did it standing up.

'Can't get pregnant if you do it like that,' he assured her, and she believed him. She still believed it a couple of years later when she fell for a baby. She didn't tell anyone for months, until one day during the last lesson at school she was doubled up with excruciating pain and began to bleed from her vagina. She was rushed to the Royal London Hospital A&E where the tiny, dead body was extracted from her womb and burned. She never saw the baby. Later, after her mum had been summoned from home, the attending doctor came to Poppy's bedside and explained that it had been touch and go whether Poppy lived. 'You were losing a lot of blood,' he said. 'Too much to survive, unless I did something drastic.'

The two women listened intently.

'I had to perform an emergency sterilisation,' he continued. 'I'm afraid you won't be able to have more children. I'm terribly sorry.'

Poppy didn't care. The short pregnancy had been a nightmare as far as she was concerned. Mum didn't say much. In fact, later she often wished that the same thing had happened to her. At least then she could have made a career, made some money, had a life. Not scratching from day to day in a thin-walled flat where every sound of the neighbour's lives could be heard through the partitions. But she would never say as much to Poppy, and felt guilty even thinking about it. She loved her, even though she was a wild girl.

Poppy didn't change much. She left school early and drifted from job to job. It wasn't that she was stupid. It just seemed that nothing much mattered except getting a couple of quid for spliff and CD's, and a few vodka and cokes at the weekends.

And then along came Joseph Barlow.

Tall, handsome, from the same Caribbean stock as her father whom she'd never known. His skin was the colour of chocolate, and the white teeth in his handsome face flashed each time he smiled, which he did often. His hair was sculpted in a high fade, and razored into strange, geometric patterns at the back of his head. He drove a black BMW with dark windows, carried a wad of cash big enough to choke a horse, dressed as if he'd just stepped out of the pages of *GQ* and wore just enough bling to be noticed without going over the top.

From the moment Poppy saw him holding court in a local pub, she was his. She didn't care that he was a gangster. If she was honest it made him all the more attractive.

They were married within a month and he paid the deposit on a luxury flat, just close enough to her mum's to keep in touch, but not close enough that she was always round.

Poppy had never been so happy. She quickly

made friends with Sadie, Kate and Niki. They often lunched together, although Niki was a rare companion in the early days, before Connie relented and allowed her a little more freedom. Poppy loved it when they did. The four beautiful women out on the town together almost stopped the traffic, and they revelled in the attention they got. Those were happy times. Until one day, out of the blue Joseph told her he wanted kids. Lots of them. Poppy told him the truth about herself, and that was when things began to go wrong.

Their sex life, which had been so passionate that they used to fuck at least twice a day, began to dwindle. One day a helpful neighbour of her mum's told Poppy over a cup of tea that she'd seen Joseph with a young girl down at Sainsbury's, buying groceries. A young, pregnant girl. Poppy didn't believe a word. Joseph, food shopping? No chance. That was her job. But once the seeds of doubt had been sown, they soon began to grow into ugly weeds. She started noticing how often he was away from home lately, and how sex had become almost non-existent. So Poppy began to follow him. She borrowed a car from a friend and tagged after him in his Beemer. It didn't take many days before he turned up at a council flat in Bow, where a pretty black girl in the later stages of pregnancy met him at the door with a passionate kiss.

After that Poppy haunted the building. She saw the girl getting bigger every day, and later, she saw the pair of them coming back from hospital in Joseph's car, complete with baby carrier. She saw the way he proudly handled the child. Bastard, she thought, as his absences became longer. She checked his credit card receipts. Fortunes spent at Mothercare. Bastard, she thought again, getting angrier.

She turned to Sadie, her best friend amongst the girls. '*He's* a bastard,' said Sadie, 'but that's men all over.'

Poppy's love, once so strong, turned to something else. Her love had been soured—poisoned by his betrayal. But she still played the part of the loving wife. Cooking Joseph's favourite curry goat with rice and peas, mixing his rum and cokes, laughing at his jokes, washing his dirty Calvins. But deep down the poison grew stronger as the love grew weaker. Poppy knew, as all women know who've been neglected by their men, that one day the worm would turn, and she would get her own back.

5

When Kate felt depressed she went shoplifting. Hoisting she called it. She'd done it all her life, and even though she could afford to buy almost anything she wanted, the thrill of nicking gave her the highs she desired in her life. Dolly had started her off when she was a kid. Dolly had been an expert shoplifter long before she married Johnny Wade, and it seemed to run in the family. Kate started as Dolly's shill when she was barely fifteen. She would cause a disturbance by faking illness, rolling about on the floor whilst Dolly got on with the business at hand. She knew that every eye in the shop would be on her, especially the men, if she showed off her knickers under a short skirt. Or else she'd walk out with the security button still attached to a garment, as Dolly did the same, and it was Kate's job to pretend she had accidentally stumbled past the security barrier as Dolly got away with the goods. It worked well. Kate always came over like butter wouldn't melt, charming both shop assistants and store detectives, and she and Dolly made quite a killing between them.

But on the whole Kate had preferred working solo. She'd visit Brent Cross or Lakeside and come home with CDs, DVDs and clothes. Anything that could be smuggled out in her handbag or up her tee-shirt.

Now as an adult, with Dolly gone, she concentrated on Oxford Street and Bond Street and the expensive boutiques between. She'd put her face on and act as if she could buy the store with her loose change, and in all the years she'd been doing it, although there'd been plenty of close calls and embarrassing moments, she'd never been nicked. She'd always managed to talk her way out of trouble, or pay up and look big. Or as a last resort, just do a runner.

That is, until one day in April that year, when everything started to unravel. Kate had assumed one of the disguises she used when on the hoist. Nothing spectacular. It was just a case of putting her hair up under a hat, wearing Prada spectacles (with clear glass instead of prescription lenses), and a Gucci trench coat with the collar up. She looked just right. A clone for her Mayfair sisters as she sauntered up and down South Molton Street, her big handbag over her shoulder and a mobile plugged into her ear. No one on the other end, but it helped allay shop assistants' fears as she nattered on to a dead line.

There was a silk blouse she fancied in one of the tiny shops, so she pointed to another item with the hand holding the phone, and as the girl behind the counter retrieved it, the blouse vanished into her bag. No security device on that one she noted. Some people were just too trusting. Herself included, as she didn't notice the handsome Asian man checking out the contents of the window behind her, and Kate into the bargain.

After declining the sweater the assistant showed her, Kate left and cut through towards Berkeley Square. All was well, or so she thought. It was then that she felt a tap on her shoulder. She turned and the Asian man was standing behind her, a smile on his face. 'Hello,' he said. 'I think you forgot something.'

Kate frowned. 'What?' she asked.

'To pay for that blouse in your bag.'

'What blouse, and what's it got to do with you?' At times like these Kate could come over all imperious, like Victoria Beckham being asked for proof of identity.

'Depends,' said the Asian man, as he reached into the inside pocket of his jacket and pulled out a leather case, which he opened to show his ID. 'Detective Sergeant Ali S. Karim,' he said. 'And you love, are nicked.'

Kate said nothing.

'Want to take a walk?' said Ali.

'I'll scream,' said Kate. 'I'll tell people you attacked me. Tried to touch me.'

'Leave it out darling,' said Ali. 'See over there.'

Kate looked round and saw a squad car parked a few yards away on the other side of the road. The cops inside were clocking the pair.

'One word from me, and you're inside that motor and on the way to the nick.'

Again, Kate said nothing in reply.

Ali had checked her out as he'd followed her from the shop. She was a beauty and no mistake, he thought. A bit rich for a copper's blood, but you never know. And he was off duty, although no copper ever was really. He didn't give a damn about an overpriced bit of *schmutter* being lifted from a shop run by a bunch of toffee-nosed white bitches who he knew would immediately assume he was on the rob if he ever went inside, simply because of the colour of his skin. Fuck 'em, he thought.

'On the other hand,' he went on. 'Maybe we could just go for a cup of coffee and sort things out between ourselves.'

There was another moment of silence, and Kate went for the latter option. He was a good looking man, and the last thing she needed that morning was a trip down West End Central. Get him on his own, and she might just be able to talk her way out of trouble again.

'Coffee, it is then,' she said after a moment, and as Ali took her arm she smiled at the two coppers in the squad car, who as one smiled back.

6

There was a cafe just round the corner. Old fashioned. It had been there since God was a boy,
avoiding the influx of Starbucks and Caffé Nero, or
whatever it was called. The plate glass window
was steamed up, and a massive Gaggia machine
hissed and spluttered behind the counter. Ali sat
Kate down at a quiet table in the corner and
ordered two cappuccinos. 'A sticky bun?' he asked,
but she ignored him and he grinned. Gotcha, he
thought.

He took their drinks over and sat opposite her.
'Right,' he said. 'You know who I am, who are
you?'

She thought of giving a false name, but he beat

her to it. 'Show me some ID,' he said, and took her bag and opened it. He ignored the silky blouse and dug deep until her found her purse thick with cash and credit cards. 'Could've paid,' he said. 'Naughty, naughty.'

He took out her driving licence, fished out his phone and made a call. 'Excuse me,' he said as he turned away. 'Police business.'

She grimaced.

He whispered into the phone, reading out the details from the document, and then was silent for a moment. 'Christ,' he said at length. 'You're joking,' as he looked at Kate with a different expression in his eyes. He snapped the phone shut eventually and said. 'You're Robbo Ellis's missus. And Johnny Wade's daughter. What the hell are you doing on the knock?'

'I like it. Gets my juices running,' she said defiantly, looking straight into his chocolate-brown eyes.

'And nicking Robbo's missus does the same for me.'

'You know him then?' she asked.

'Every copper in the Met knows him,' he said. 'But not personally. But some do I'm sure, from what I've heard.' And he made the international sign for money by rubbing his right thumb over the fingers of his right hand.

'So what?' she asked, ignoring it. 'It's me that pinched the blouse.'

'So you admit it?'

'In here. Not at the nick.'

'Been there before, have you?'

'Only to report a lost dog.'

'Did they find it?'

'Yes. As a matter of fact.'

'See. We are good for something.'

'Sometimes,' she replied.

He smiled, and she had to admit the smile did something for her. 'So what am I going to do with you?' he asked.

'Better make up your mind, or I'm off out of here.'

'I could cuff you and read you your rights. I bet Robbo wouldn't be pleased if he heard about that.'

'I doubt that he would. But then I doubt that he's going to.'

'Meaning?'

'Meaning that instead of being banged up in a cell round the corner, I'm sitting here in this charming, if rather retro establishment having a delicious beverage with a strange foreign man.'

'I'm not foreign,' he interrupted. 'I was born in Croydon.'

'That's foreign to me,' she went on. 'And believe me if he saw us now he'd have something to say about it. He doesn't like me talking to strange men.'

'Is that why he hits you?' he said.

'What do you mean?'

He plucked off the glasses she was still wearing. 'If I'm not mistaken, and I rarely am,' he said. 'You recently had a black eye. I can see you've loaded on the slap, but it's still a bit yellow.'

'Clever aren't you?'

'Top of my class in the sergeant's exam.'

'So why *haven't* you nicked me?'

'Paperwork. I'm down here looking for a present for my sister's birthday. It's my day off, and I don't want to spend it in a strange nick processing you.'

'So can I go?'

'You haven't finished your coffee, and it's almost lunchtime, and we're both alone. Fancy a bite?'

She looked at him closely again. Handsome. A bit flash. Well built. And she'd never been with a coloured bloke. And she was lonely and sad and fucked up and fucked off with her life. 'Curry?' she said, and for a moment his face went hard until he realised she was pulling his leg.

'There's a hotel across the road,' he said. 'I've heard the dining-room is one of the best in London. Care to give it a try?'

'Expensive?' she asked.

'Yes.'

'And you're paying?'

'Of course.'

'Well, I suppose it's one way of getting the taxes we pay back.'

'You and Robbo pay tax?'

'Don't be silly. Remember Al Capone?'

'What about him?'

'Got away with murder for years, then went inside for tax evasion. Stupid, yeah?'

Beautiful, and quick too, thought Ali. 'I remember,' he said. 'Want to go?'

She nodded.

So they did.

7

———◆———

They finished their drinks, left the cafe and crossed
the road to where the hotel stood behind a curved
driveway. The doorman touched the brim of his
top hat and wished them a good afternoon, and
Ali responded with the same. The automatic doors
swished open and he allowed Kate to enter first.
Once inside in the ornately decorated lobby, he
went to reception to enquire about a table for
lunch whilst Kate looked around nervously,
praying she wouldn't see anyone she knew. She
was tempted to turn on her heel and run, but she
felt strangely attracted to the Asian man. She
didn't play away as a rule, like Sadie did. She was
too afraid of Robbo's temper for one thing, and

apart from that it wasn't in her nature. But the thought of the young copper touching her had, as she'd previously said about shop lifting, got her juices running.

He turned from the desk with a smile. 'Table for two, at one,' he said. 'Fancy a drink first?'

'I thought you people didn't drink.'

'Us people, as you so kindly call us, are a mixed and interesting race. I'm not a Muslim. I'm a copper, and I drink.'

'Good. A drink it is then.'

They followed the signs to the cocktail bar, which was dimly lit and almost empty. Kate sat at a table and Ali said, 'What do you fancy?'

You, thought Kate, but said, 'gin and tonic, large one. Ice and a slice.'

He went to the bar and ordered the drinks, and Kate watched his firm, muscular arse. Better and better, she thought.

When he returned with two glasses beaded with moisture, Kate took out her cigarettes. 'Do you mind?' she asked.

'Not only don't I mind, I'll ponce one of yours,' he replied.

'All the vices, I see,' she said.

He smiled, a dangerous, reckless, smile. 'You'd better believe it.'

'This is dangerous,' said Kate when they were

both smoking. 'If Robbo knew...' She didn't finish the sentence.

'Are *you* going to tell him?'

'Christ no.'

'That's all right then.'

'I really shouldn't be here.'

'What, and miss lunch?'

'Even that.'

'I believe it's shepherd's pie and cabbage at the station Thursdays.' Ali said, arching an eyebrow.

'Is that a threat?' she asked.

'As if I would.'

'I believe you might.'

'Come on Kate, enjoy your drink. They'll bring us a menu in a minute. No shepherds pie and cabbage here.'

Indeed there wasn't. The restaurant was as good as Ali had promised. Recently taken over by a famous TV chef, the menu was something called modern British, which seemed to mean old-fashioned food at inflated prices. They chose a mixed array of dishes from the huge menu brought by a young woman in a white blouse and black skirt, and at one precisely were led to a table in a secluded corner.

An hour and a half passed quickly. Kate found Ali easy to talk to in a way that Robbo had never been, and the more she drank, the more she found herself wondering what he would look like naked. As they were served coffee and liqueurs, Ali asked, 'Having a good time?'

Kate smiled. 'Yes.'

'What now?'

'What do you have in mind?'

'Well, you could go home, forget all about me, and breathe a sigh of relief that you aren't up for a criminal record. How have you managed to avoid that by the way?'

'Blind luck?'

'I don't believe it. You're too smart.'

'If you say so.'

'I do.'

'Or?' she asked.

'Or what?'

'What if I don't want to go home?'

'Well. I enquired about rooms. There's a nice double up for grabs.'

'Confident, aren't you?' she said, mock-glaring at him, but smiling.

'It's in my nature.'

'And in the room?'

'Well I imagine there's a bed, and a minibar, and…'

'And?'

'And we could get to know each other better,' he said.

'You're propositioning me.'
'I thought that was obvious.'
'Do I look that easy?'
'Not at all. If you did I wouldn't bother.'
'Is that a compliment?'
'If you like.'
'I like. Book the room.'
So he did.

8

The room was on the fourth floor overlooking the street. Ali drew the curtains back and looked down at the traffic, running silent because of the triple glazing. Kate stood at the door, suddenly shy and unsure why she was there. Too much booze with lunch, she thought, and almost ran out again.

'Nervous?' asked Ali as he turned to face her across the huge bed that dominated the room.

She nodded.

'Don't be. No pressure. You can go if you want.'

'And stiff you for the room?'

'I can afford it.'

'Take backhanders do you?'

'None of your business. But I mean it Kate. If you want to go you can.'

'I don't want to go, but…'

'But what?'

'If Robbo even guessed,' she said, looking nervously at the door.

'This is not you then?'

'No. Far from it. I'm a good girl.'

'Except for the blouse.'

'Do we have to talk about that?'

'No. All forgotten. Well?'

'Did you say something about a minibar?'

'That's my girl.'

'Not yet, but maybe…'

She moved into the room, dropped her bag on the floor, pulled off her hat and let her long, red hair cascade down around her shoulders.

Ali was mesmerised. 'God,' he said. 'You're even more beautiful than I thought.'

'Thank you, kind sir.'

'I don't believe this,' said Ali. 'Am I dreaming?'

'I don't think so. I don't believe it either.'

'But here we are.'

'So?'

'So?'

'So do something about it.'

Suddenly they were in each other's arms kissing madly, and they rolled onto the bed tearing at each other's clothes. Kate was amazed at the ferocity of her passion, and she felt that she might faint with lust as Ali ripped off her underwear, then his own, to reveal his long, hard penis. 'You're beautiful too. Such a fucking gorgeous man,' said Kate as she reached for him, then put his cock into her mouth.

Ali lay back as she sucked on him. 'Stop,' he said. 'I don't want to come.'

Kate's response was to suck harder, as Ali tried breathlessly protesting again.

She let him go for a moment. 'Shut up Ali,' she said. 'You're mine now.'

Ali knew when he was beaten, and helplessly lay back on the bedcover looking at the ceiling as she brought him to a climax. 'You bitch,' he said, smiling at her, his face sexily flushed. 'That was too quick.'

'Plenty of time sexy boy, I want some fun too.'

They lay together in each others arms, until Ali roused himself and found a bottle of champagne in the fridge. 'I don't make a habit of spending my afternoons in bed with strange men.' said Kate. 'I don't suppose you came prepared?'

'I told you, I was looking for a present for my sister,' said Ali. 'I really didn't think anything like this was going to happen.'

'Then be careful,' said Kate as he popped the

cork and filled two glasses. 'We don't want any little accidents.'

'I'll do my best,' said Ali.

'Make sure you do.'

They spent the rest of the afternoon making love. Kate was in a dream as she came time and time again, something that had never happened with Robbo. She was overwhelmed by the strength of her desire for Ali and felt like she imagined men did during sex, fucking Ali harder until they were both panting with exhaustion. Robbo had been the only man she had known sexually before that strange afternoon of passion. Passion that she'd never felt for her husband. She'd discussed sex with her friends, and read dozens if not hundreds of articles about it in *Cosmopolitan* and *Marie Claire*, but had half believed that what she'd heard and read was sheer fantasy. Pipe dreams invented out of frustration. But suddenly under Ali's practised fingers and lips the fantasy came to life, and she knew that life with Robbo would never be the same again.

At last she looked at her watch and saw it was almost five. 'Christ, I've got to get back,' she said.

'Don't go,' said Ali.

'I have to, sweetheart.'

'Are you driving?'

'Yes. My car's in a garage in Berkeley Square. Thank Christ, it is, otherwise it would've been towed away by now. What about you?'

'Tube. I'm just a poor copper remember.'

'Not so poor in bed. By the way what does the "S" stand for?'

'Sex god,' he replied with a laugh.

'You can say that again babe.'

'Will I see you again?' he asked, suddenly serious.

'Do you want to?'

'What do you think? Do you?'

'Absolutely. But we'll have to be careful.'

'We will, I promise.'

'If this ever gets out, we're dead, you know that.'

'Not necessarily. I'm a copper.'

'So? Do you think Robbo gives a fuck about that?'

'He wouldn't dare.'

'You'd be amazed what he'd do.'

'I'm willing to risk it.'

'Me too.' She got up from the wrecked bed and began to get dressed. Ali watched in admiration, his cock growing hard again.

'Down boy,' she said. 'Save it for another time. Or your girlfriend.'

'Not guilty,' he said.

'Good-looking bloke like you? Bet your mum's got you married off to some nice, sweet girl already.'

'Not guilty again.'

'I bet that's what you tell all your conquests.'

'It's the truth.' And strangely enough, it was.

'I'm going to shoot off,' she said. 'Home in time for dinner.'

'I'm jealous.'

'Good. But you shouldn't be.'

'How do we keep in touch?'

'Give me your mobile number. I'll call you. Don't ever call me. I know you can get numbers, but don't. I mean it. If you do, it's over.'

'OK.' He pulled his notebook from his pocket and scratched down his number with the pen from the bedside table.

She pulled on her hat, mac and glasses, retrieved her bag, pushed the piece of paper into one of the inside pockets, and leant down and kissed him hard on the mouth. 'Thanks for a great time. I can hardly walk.'

'Good.'

'I'll be in touch.'

'Please do.'

And with one more kiss she was gone. Back to her car, and her husband in Essex, feeling better than she'd felt for years.

9

———⟫◦⟪———

So the seeds of deceit were being sown. Poppy had to work hard at keeping her feelings for Joseph hidden, Sadie kept working her way through the young men she needed more and more whilst Kate, usually so poised and assured, was in the first flush of a tumultuous affair that made her feel like an oversexed teenager.

Niki concentrated on keeping fit and brushing up on her martial arts skills. As a child her father had introduced her to Judo, Karate, and even more exotic forms of hand to hand combat. Niki had taken to it like a duck to water, and after her father died, her grandfather had continued her education. Back in Russia she'd watched Bruce

Lee films until the tape on the video wore thin, but Connie had no idea of her expertise. In the mornings, when he either lay in bed, or was off on some nefarious task, Niki would pull on a shapeless track suit, pull her hair back into a band and go for a run round the Isle of Dogs ending up at Millwall Park, where she would practice her katas for hours until her body was totally limber, and the perspiration poured down her back. She was tough. Tough enough that, when the crunch with Connie came, as she knew one day it would, she could take care of herself—under any circumstances.

One morning in spring as she was practicing her moves, three men left Island Gardens DLR station and made their way to the park. Each of them carried a striped off-licence bag full of cans of lager and it was obvious they'd already drained several.

They spotted Niki straight away, standing stock still amongst the dog walkers and commuters hurrying to work, and decided she was just the thing for a bit of entertainment, before getting down to the serious business of getting thoroughly rat-arsed.

'Oi love,' said the biggest of the trio, an obese barrel of a man in a West Ham shirt and dirty jeans. 'What you doing then?'

Niki, engrossed in practising her deadly karate

moves, didn't even hear his question.

'He's talking to you,' said the second man, a weaselly little runt with a pockmarked face, wearing a fake leather jacket and combat pants.

Once again Niki didn't hear.

'You cunt,' spat the third. Well built, but rapidly turning to fat, he nonetheless thought himself a wow with the ladies, despite his repellent body odour.

His words got through to Niki's brain, and she turned towards them. 'What did you say?' she asked, her accent hard in the morning air.

'Fuck me,' said the first one. 'A bleedin' foreigner. What are you then? A fuckin' asylum seeker on the scrounge?'

Considering none of the trio had done a day's work in decades seemed to make no difference to his righteous indignation. Years of reading reactionary tabloids had convinced him that anyone with a foreign accent was only in the country to steal the benefits he received from the state, and that were his natural right.

'What do you want?' asked Niki. She was confused, about why the men were picking on her.

'He wants to know what you're up to, you dumb fucking bitch,' snarled Weasel.

A native east-ender might have come up with some quick remark, or possibly told them to piss off and mind their own business. Even if they were mob-handed, and well on the way to being drunk and disorderly.

'I'm practising,' said Niki. She wasn't afraid, just a bit perplexed by their attention.

'Practising what?' asked Pock-marks. He was beginning to enjoy the sport. Nothing like three men against a lone woman to add a little spice to the day. His little firm were feared in many a boozer from Hackney to Limehouse, and barred from most for bad behaviour. But one on one was not their idea of fun.

'Martial arts.'

'Fucking *Kung-Fu*,' said Weasel. '*Glasshopper*.'

This piece of wit caused them all to laugh nastily.

Niki didn't know what he was talking about, as *Kung-Fu* had never reached Russian TV in the Seventies.

She looked confused again. 'What?' she asked.

'Fucking ignorant Gyppo,' said the first man around a mouthful of Stella Artois, and he went to push her down.

It was his second mistake of the day. The first was getting up.

Niki swayed away from his touch, and moved within reach of the Lady-Killer who grabbed her by the shoulder. Another bad idea in a lifetime of them.

Niki turned sharply and roughly pulled her shoulder away.

Weasel laughed. 'What's the matter with you two?' he said, 'She's just a girl,' and he tried to stuff the hand not holding the can up her tee-shirt.

It was this clumsy attempt to touch her that filled her with rage. She bounced on her Nike trainers, and appeared to simply touch the man three times. Once on each shoulder, and once in the solar plexus. Weasel dropped like a stone, his can erupting foam, as Niki spun on the balls of her feet and delivered a kick to the Barrel Man's crotch. His scream froze passers-by as he doubled up and fell to his knees, his beer joining Weasel's on the grass.

The Lady-Killer was thinking twice about what to do next. Who the fuck was this woman, and what had gone wrong with the day?

Almost as an afterthought Niki chopped him beneath his nose, and his two front teeth, of which he was inordinately proud, were forced down his throat. When the second chop hit his Adam's apple, they were projected out of his mouth in a gout of blood.

The third strike was at his right knee, and as he lost all feeling in his leg, he too hit the deck.

'Don't ever touch me again,' said Niki, to their prone bodies. 'And don't come back.'

With that, and under the gaze of half a dozen

people in the park she set off for home, knowing
that she'd have to find somewhere else to exercise
from then on.

10

Sadie kept on with her life as usual. But she knew something was badly wrong. Eddie had become more and more withdrawn as the days went by, as it got closer to his court appearance. Even the forty grand seemed to have evaporated away. But when Sadie tried to talk to him he just ignored her, or left the room, put a DVD into his home cinema set-up and closed the door on her. Or on even more occasions lately, he left the house, drove away, and didn't return for hours.

She was more worried than she'd admit. He'd been up in front of a jury before and always had a good result. Not guilty. But this time seemed different and she didn't like it. Also, she had noticed there were a lot of lengthy phone calls being conducted in hushed tones. When she asked about them, he just told her, 'Don't worry babe.' But the more she heard the words, the more she did.

But as her home life seemed to be falling apart, her sex life was on a roll. She had recently met a wild young man in a wine bar in Ilford. He was tall and handsome, about twenty-five, single, and up for it. Just the way Sadie liked her boys. He ran a stall in the market selling DVDs, and as she was sitting, sipping on a glass of Pinot Grigiot, he slumped down in the chair opposite and said, 'This seat taken?'

'Looks like it is now.'

'Not if you've got a geezer at the bar.'

'You know damn well I haven't. You've been screwing me for the last ten minutes.'

'Only in my head.'

'And that's where it'll stay.'

'Spoilsport.'

Sadie smiled at that. She liked a bit of verbal fencing before she got down to business with a new man.

The man took the smile as a green light, and went on. 'So what's your name then, love?'

'None of your business.'

'Don't be like that. It's a beautiful day, and you're beautiful too.'

'How often do you spin that line?'

'No, I mean it. My name's Spencer by the way. My friends call me Spence.'

'Hello *Spencer*.'

'I can tell you're a harsh woman, but I like that.'

'Would you like my drink in your face?'

He laughed. 'I don't think so. I just had this jacket cleaned. Well, if I've offended you I'm sorry. Just passing the time of day. I'll be off. Half the day gone and not a penny earned. Sure I can't top you up before I go?'

She pretended to weigh up the question. 'Go on then,' she said. 'Pinot Grigiot.'

'A fine choice.'

He went to the bar and returned with wine for her and a bottle of Becks for himself. 'So what *is* your name?' he asked.

'Sadie,' she relented.

'See how easy that was.'

'Don't get any ideas.'

'Ideas?' he said, grinning suggestively.

'About me being easy.'

'Fair enough. So Sadie, what do you do, apart from sitting around in bars in the morning, drinking wine?'

'I've got a private income.'

'Yeah?'

'Yeah. My husband's.'

'I noticed the ring.' It wasn't difficult, as the diamond in her engagement ring rivalled the rock of Gibraltar. 'He must be making a few bob.'

Thinking of the upcoming court date, Sadie wasn't so sure. 'He does all right,' she replied.

'What business is he in?'

'Does it matter?'

'Just making conversation.'

'Sure. Sorry. Let's not talk about him.'

'Fine by me. Let's talk about you then.'

'Not much to say really,' Sadie answered, icily.

Spencer, not picking up on Sadie's reluctance to talk about herself, pressed on. 'I don't believe that for a minute.'

'Yeah, yeah, yeah.'

'I mean it.'

'Sure you do.'

'Honest.'

That was the last thing Sadie wanted-honesty. All she wanted and needed was a good fuck and a lot of lies. She was used to that. At least, the lies part. 'Do you do this a lot?' she asked.

'What?'

'Chat up married women.'

'Yeah, I'm an expert.'

'I can believe that.'

They both smiled at that, and Sadie knew she'd

made a new conquest. In fact she'd known that since he'd come in. The question remained, what to do with him.

11

'You got a place?' asked Sadie.

Spence looked surprised. He hadn't expected things to go this fast when he'd spotted this tasty, older woman sitting in the wine bar.

'Yes. But it's not much.'

'I didn't expect much. Not from the state of you,' said Sadie.

'Charming.' He was wearing a suede jacket and jeans, with Timberland boots, a Hawaiian shirt, with a silk scarf knotted loosely round his neck. He thought he looked the business.

'Pikey chic,' said Sadie. 'All you need is a pair of Elvis sunglasses, and you'd be perfect for karaoke.'

'I can see I'm going to have trouble with you.'

'Not if you behave yourself.'

Spencer felt a trifle intimidated. He was used to being the one in control with the birds he met on his stall in the market, or in the clubs and pubs he frequented, but he'd never met anyone like Sadie before.

Not many men had.

She finished her drink before he'd finished his, collected her things and stood up. 'Come on then,' she said. 'Get a move on. I haven't got all day.'

He gulped some more beer, then left the bottle on the table and followed her to the door, where she stood until he realised what she wanted, and opened it for her. She smiled an acknowledgement and went outside.

'Where's your car?' she said. 'I assume you do have a car.'

'Van. For stock, you know?'

'Barrow-boy. What do you sell?'

'DVDs.'

'Pirates, I suppose?'

'Sometimes.'

'Where's the stall?'

'In the square. I haven't set up yet. Fancied a livener. Best business's lunch time, and evenings.'

'Looks like it's your day off then. Where's it parked?'

'On a meter round the corner.' He pointed, and

she set off before he could say another word. He followed like an obedient puppy. Just the way Sadie liked things. 'Where's *your* motor?' he asked as they went.

'I came by cab. Can't be bothered looking for parking round here,' she said.

The van was a battered white Transit sitting low on its springs at the back. Sadie waited whilst Spence opened the passenger door and she wrinkled her nose at the interior of the cab, it being full of McDonald's boxes and cans and sandwich wrappers. 'Sorry,' said Spence. 'I wasn't expecting giving anyone a ride.'

'I thought that was my job?' said Sadie raising an eyebrow.

Spence pulled rubbish out of the passenger side and dumped it at the kerb, Sadie got in, and he went and opened the driver's door and nervously got behind the wheel. The old vehicle wheezed into life and he drove away. Their destination was a short run to a dilapidated council block. Sadie shook her head in disbelief. 'What?' said Spence.

'Nothing. I hope it's better inside.'

It was, but not much. The flat was on the top floor, one bedroom, living room, kitchen and bathroom. The furniture was minimal. Most of the living room was taken up by a plasma screen TV with all the trimmings including surround sound,

DVD recorder and Sky-Plus box, a sagging sofa, and a rubbish strewn coffee table. 'For work,' explained Spence, pointing at the TV. 'I have to watch the stuff.'

'Bet you love watching porn on that big TV,' said Sadie. 'Got anything to drink?'

Sadie was drinking more and more these days. And the reason she came by cab was to avoid being nicked. It was expensive, but what the hell?

'Beer, scotch, vodka.'

'Vodka ice,' she said.

'The fridge is busted.'

'Jesus, Spence, you sure know how to treat a girl.'

A lot of Spence's cockiness had been knocked out of him by then. Once again, just as Sadie wanted it. She was always the boss in these assignations. She started them, and when she was bored, she finished them. But she didn't want to totally kill his confidence. She wanted a man, not a mouse. So she smiled. 'Don't worry about it. Warm vodka will do fine.'

He went out to the kitchen and she heard water running and he returned with a bottle of Stoli and two clean glasses. Whilst he was gone she'd shifted papers and clothes off the sofa and sat down. He put the bottle and glasses on the coffee table in front of the TV and emptied an ashtray into an already full waste bin. 'Sorry about this.' he said. 'I wasn't expecting visitors here either.'

'No problem,' replied Sadie. 'I don't see the hand of a woman here.'

'No,' he said. 'No girlfriend at the moment. Just, you know, the occasional…'

'One-night stand,' Sadie finished for him. 'Or one-day stand.'

He smiled. 'Something like that.'

He poured two drinks and she sipped at the oily tasting liquid, feeling it burn the back of her throat. 'Right Spence,' she said. 'Where's the bedroom?'

12

The bedroom wasn't much better. It contained just a mattress on a box spring, with a duvet tossed untidily on it, and a chair covered in clothes. 'Not the Ritz is it?' said Sadie.

'I usually don't ask people back,' said Spence.

'I'm not surprised. But it'll do, I suppose.' She walked over to the window and looked down at the scruffy grass in front of the flats, and the old bangers abandoned at the side of the road. This could've been me, she thought. And worse, it still could be if Eddie goes down. This was not a good thought, so she dismissed it as she pulled the ill-fitting curtains together and turned round in the dim light that remained. 'So what's it to be

Spence?' she asked. 'How do you like it?'

Spence liked it rough, which was fine by Sadie. He also had a good stock of ribbed Durex, which also fitted her bill.

But first she undressed slowly, taking her time, and enjoying the effect she was having on him. Her blouse came off to expose the La Perla lacy black bra beneath, then her pencil skirt dropped to the floor exposing the matching panties. She could see Spence appreciated the show as his cock grew large in his trousers. 'Like what you see?' she asked.

He nodded, the breath catching in his throat.

She went towards him and reached for his crotch. 'I thought you might be worth knowing,' she said, feeling the hardness beneath her fingers.

She pushed his jacket off his shoulders, undid the scarf and tossed it aside, and began to unbutton his shirt to expose his hard chest and six-pack. 'Work out, do you?' she asked.

'When I can.'

'Work out on me then,' she whispered as she kissed him on the mouth, her tongue forcing his lips open.

He picked her up easily and put onto the bed as they carried on kissing and he pushed her bra up around her neck to expose her creamy breasts.

'Oh, yes,' he breathed.

'You like?'

'I love.'

'There's a good boy.'

As he kissed and sucked her nipples, Sadie unbuttoned his flies and tugged his jeans and pants down allowing his cock to spring up, long and hard.

Sadie ran her mouth down his chest and belly and took his prick in her mouth. 'God,' he said.

She cupped his balls as he took off her panties too, and he put his fingers into her cleft which was already hot and wet.

'Yes, oh yes, Spence,' she breathed. 'That's so good.'

'Let me in you,' he said, and she pushed her knickers off, rolled onto her back and opened her legs wide.

He wrestled off his boots, tore open a condom packet with his teeth and rolled it on, then quickly mounted her, his trousers around his ankles. It was awkward, but Sadie didn't care as the long length of him pushed deep inside her.

'Oh fuck,' she shouted as her long nails cut into his back. 'Oh fuck, you dirty fucker.'

He covered her mouth with his as he pumped her hard, and she could already feel her orgasm building.

'Harder, you bastard, harder,' she ordered, but his tongue was halfway down her throat, and he probably didn't hear, or care, but harder he went until she pulled her head back and screamed, and he shot his load into the rubber.

They lay together for a few minutes, both breathing hard, before Spence withdrew, removed the condom and dropped it on the floor.

'Well, that's the best thing I've ever got from Ilford market,' said Sadie, breathlessly.

13

Which just left Poppy. The anger at Joseph's betrayal cut her deeper with every day. She paced the floor of their flat disinterested at the luxury in which she lived, knowing that he was spending more and more time with his baby mother and the child. She felt that she had nowhere to turn. Her mother was a lost cause who just sat indoors all day drinking sweet wine, smoking the cheapest tipped king size cigarettes she could find, reading the *Daily Mirror* and watching *The Jeremy Kyle Show* on ITV. So once more she turned to Sadie. Poppy would ring her and talk for hours. Sadie actually welcomed the calls, as they took her mind off her own problems. She was still seeing Spence, but was becoming bored with his squalid lifestyle, and knew it wouldn't be long before she dumped him.

'Let's meet up Poppy darlin',' she said one bright morning a week before Eddie's court day. 'Let's just you and me have lunch, maybe do a bit of shopping.'

'Where?' asked Poppy.

'West End,' said Sadie. 'Let's push the boat out. I'll come in on the train, cab it from Liverpool Street. It's been ages since I've done that. We'll get a bit pissed and spend some of those sods ill-gottens.'

'Sounds good to me,' said Poppy. 'Serves the bastards right.'

They arranged to meet in Selfridges in the wine bar next to the food hall the next day at eleven. Poppy was early and mooched around the lingerie department, bitterly remembering when Joseph was interested in her underwear.

Sadie arrived fifteen minutes late as Polly was sitting at the bar staring into a glass of bottled water. 'Sorry love,' she said, giving the younger woman a big hug. 'Traffic's murder, and I swear my cabbie didn't know his arse from his elbow.'

Despite herself, Poppy had to smile. Sadie's bitching never failed to cheer her up.

'What's that you're drinking?' asked Sadie.

'Water.'

'Do leave off. You know what fishes do in it?'

'This is supposed to come from the mountains of Mourne or somewhere,' said Poppy, peering at the bottle.

'Bollocks. Water's water. Come on love, we ain't here for a wake, though you look like you might be,' and she called for a bottle of Pinot Blanc and two glasses.

They moved to a table, and despite one or two glances Sadie fired up a Silk Cut. 'Fuck 'em,' she said looking round. 'The bloody prices they charge I'm allowed a fag.'

Poppy shook her head. She could tell it was going to be one of those days, and she felt that she deserved one too.

When the wine was poured and the cigarettes were on the go, Sadie said. 'So what's he done now? You look like you've lost a fiver and found a tanner.'

'Just the same,' said Poppy. 'He's never home. Always round that bird's flat playing mummies and daddies.'

'It's the way of the world darlin',' said Sadie. 'Whatever they can't have they want. Lucky Eddie don't have a fatherly bone in his body. 'Cos I sure never wanted a bunch of screaming kids hanging around me.'

'Never!'

'Never my love. Think of my figure. 'Cos if I don't no one else ever will.'

'You still seeing that bloke?' asked Poppy.

'Shh honey,' said Sadie. 'Walls have ears.' Then she laughed. 'Him and a few others.'

'God, if Eddie ever…'

'He's only interested in his case,' said Sadie. 'It could be three in the bed, and he'd never notice.'

Poppy laughed. 'So what's happening with that? Joe never talks to me any more.'

'You think I know? Eddie never talks to me either.'

'Let's drink to the fuckers then,' said Poppy. 'May they rot in hell.'

They raised their glasses and bashed them together. 'Fuck 'em,' said Sadie.

After the bottle was finished they left the store and went looking for food. 'What do you fancy?' asked Poppy. 'The Ivy?'

'That's like a greasy spoon with celebs,' said Sadie. 'Fuck it, let's go Chinese.'

They went to their favourite restaurant, The Princess Garden. The waiting staff were all young, beautiful women wearing traditional outfits but with the skirts split up almost to their knickers. All the better to charm the businessmen who used the place at lunch. Sadie marched in like she owned the place and demanded a table although they hadn't booked. And she got one.

She looked at the waitresses as they went quietly about their business. 'Us women,' she said. 'We're mugged off whoever we are.'

They ordered a selection of food, another bottle of wine and Sadie sat back in her seat and lit another cigarette. 'So come on Poppy,' she said. 'Tell me all the latest. I know you're dying to.'

14

After the first course of mixed *hors d'ouvres* was served and the wine was open, Poppy said, 'I don't think I can go on like this much longer. He's never home, and when he is, he doesn't talk to me. We don't make love, we don't do anything but sit and look at TV. And he can't wait to get away to that bitch and his little bastard.'

'Poppy,' said Sadie, picking at the food on her plate. 'We've been through this a hundred times. You can't keep torturing yourself. Shit happens. I'm in the same boat more or less, with this bloody case coming up. Eddie never tells me anything either. It's the nature of the beast as they say. You've got to get over it.'

'I can't.'

'You can. You're not the first woman this has happened to, and you won't be the last, believe me. If it's that bad, leave.'

'I can't do that either. I hate him, but I love him too. I've always loved him and I always will.'

'Then stay. You've got everything you need. A nice place, money.'

'That's nothing.'

'Tell that to some poor cow on benefits living in a slum.'

'Like my mum you mean.'

'If you like.' Then she realised what she'd said. 'Sorry doll, you know I didn't mean that about your mum.'

'I know Sade. But it hurts me so much.' She started to cry silently, and Sadie handed her a tissue to dry the tears.

'Men will always hurt you in the end, one way or another,' said Sadie, and put her hand over Poppy's for comfort.

'You do all right,' said Poppy, when she'd composed herself a bit.

'Do I? You'd be surprised,' replied Sadie.

'You've got your bloke.'

'What, Eddie? He's as bad as Joe. Like I just said. He's never around. Always in a filthy mood. You know, I think he's going down. And I think he knows it.'

'Getaway. With his brief? No chance. He's a genius.'

'Then why is Eddie so worried?'

'He's just got the jitters. It's next week isn't it?'

'Tuesday.'

'I'll be there for you. We'll all be there for you and Eddie. He's a diamond. Never said a word about the others.'

'That's his way. And thanks.'

'For what?'

'For being a mate.'

'You've been more than a mate to me Sade. I don't know what I'd do without you.'

Sadie smiled. 'Come on then girl. Eat up. My treat, and the duck here's to die for.'

'I don't think I'm that hungry, and I've got to watch my weight.'

'For Joe?'

'Yeah, you're right. Pass the damn noodles.'

As they sat in the restaurant, something began to niggle at Sadie's brain, and for once she let it grow. She looked at Poppy, and thought of Kate and Niki and herself. Four women trapped in lives none of them wanted. Four capable women who allowed their men to rule them. To walk all over them and treat them like dirt. And the beginnings of a plan began to form.

'What you thinking?' asked Poppy as she cleared her plate and laid her chopsticks on the side.

'Nothing much,' said Sadie. 'Just what I'm going to have for pudding.'

15

Tuesday rolled around, and Eddie had the runs. 'I can't get off the bloody toilet,' he shouted as Sadie got his clothes ready for court.

'There's some Diarid tablets in the medicine cupboard,' she shouted through the door of the en-suite. 'That'll sort you.'

'Fucking hell,' he moaned. 'I don't fucking believe this. Fucking Diarid, what's all that about?'

'Calm down love,' she said. 'You'll only make it worse.'

She had laid out the new Hugo Boss suit he'd bought for the occasion. Eight-hundred quid's worth of single-breasted navy blue wool and mohair. 'Got to put on a show for the jury,' he'd said when they'd gone down to Bond Street to pick it out.

Eventually he came out of the bathroom. 'My ring feels like it's on fire,' he said.

'I told you not to have curry last night.'

'I fancied a ruby. Didn't know it'd go right through.'

'It's stress,' she said. 'Those pills'll work. Give 'em time.'

'I fucking hope so. Fucking stress. You don't know what stress is.'

Don't I? she thought. But she said nothing.

He padded across the bedroom floor in his underwear and socks, plucked a new white shirt off its hanger and slipped it on. He knotted a navy blue knitted silk tie, put on his new trousers and highly polished, black Italian leather loafers. Pulling on the jacket he asked, 'How do I look?'

He was pale and had lost weight since he bought the suit, and as Sadie looked him over she felt a stab of pity for him. 'You look like a million,' she said.

She was already dressed herself. A black Dolce and Gabbana suit, white blouse unbuttoned at the throat, black tights and black Jimmy Choos. She wasn't about to let the side down either.

Eddie looked her over. 'Diamond,' he said. 'Always looking good Sade. You never let me down.'

Except when I'm in bed with a geezer thought Sadie, but once again she was silent.

'You fit then?' asked Eddie. 'The car'll be here in a minute. Driver sent me a text when I was in the khazi. Go down and open the gates, there's a doll.'

Sadie did as he asked, went downstairs and operated the gizmo that opened the front gates, and a black Beemer with black mirrored windows crawled up the drive. The driver jumped out and stood waiting. She went to the door. 'Won't be a minute darlin',' she said. 'Have a fag why don'cha?'

He took out a packet of Bensons and lit up, looking relieved. He was a local boy who knew of Eddie Ross's reputation and wanted to do nothing to upset him. 'I'd offer you a cuppa,' said Sadie. 'But we don't want to be late do we?'

'No problem Mrs Ross,' said the driver. 'Now do you want me to wait at the court? My guv'nor wasn't clear.'

'You're ours for the day sweetheart,' said Sadie. 'It's up to you. We've got your mobile. We should be out by four. You do what you want. Just be there when we leave. I expect there'll be press about and we don't want to be standing outside the Bailey with our thumbs up our arses waiting for you.'

'No chance,' said the driver. 'I'll be there. My name's Tom by the way.'

'OK, Tom,' said Sadie. 'Just make sure you're

waiting. My old man's on a short fuse today.'

I bet he is, thought Tom who had read about the case in the papers. 'Count on me,' he said. 'I've done this sort of thing before.'

'Did they have a result?'

'Always,' said Tom. 'Just like Mr Ross will.'

'I hope you're fucking right,' she said.

Eddie appeared at the door. 'All right driver?' he said.

'Ready anytime you are sir.'

'Let's go then.'

Sadie went back inside and got her handbag, locked up tight, and joined Eddie in the back seat of the motor. Tom got behind the wheel and they drove off, the gates of the house closing behind them with the metallic clang of prison doors.

16

All was quiet at the law courts however when they arrived. No journalists or cameras about as Tom dropped Sadie and Eddie off, promising to keep his phone on and charged, ready to return at a moment's notice. 'This could take days,' said Eddie. 'But you never know. Something might happen to their main witness,' he said, menace implied behind his calm words.

Tom felt a cold chill, but showed no emotion. 'Good luck Mr Ross, Mrs Ross,' he said as he ushered them out of the BMW. 'I'll see you later.'

They went inside the imposing building, topped with the statue of blind justice that Eddie gave a sardonic look.

He reported to the bailiff and was led off to the cells by court officers, whilst Sadie went looking for the rest of the crew.

She found Kate sipping from a Starbucks coffee cup. 'How you holding up?' she asked.

'Eddie's got the jitters,' replied Sadie. 'Who's about?'

'Everyone. They're outside having a fag. They'll be back in a minute. What time is Eddie on?'

'Soon.'

The others wandered in in dribs and drabs. The men were wearing pressed suits and clean shirts and ties, looking more like a convention of businessmen than a gang of villains, and the women were dolled up for a day at the races, with more Gina high heels and Fendi handbags than an episode of *Sex And The City*. 'Christ,' said Sadie when they were all gathered together. 'What time's the wedding?'

Then Eddie's case was called.

Sitting up in the spectator's gallery the court looked smaller than she imagined. Big though he was, Eddie was dwarfed by the two huge warders as he stood in the dock to hear the charges against him.

The day went badly. The witnesses for the prosecution were wheeled out and led through their carefully rehearsed evidence. The driver of the hijacked truck, his mate who'd been badly beaten, bystanders and coppers. The evidence was overwhelming. It should have been a simple job. Something the chaps could deal with blindfolded. The Mail were stupid. They never learned that everywhere there were sharp eyes watching for cash on the move. Sharp eyes that saw a pattern and sold to the likes of Eddie. The vans moved thousands, sometimes hundreds of thousands of pounds to branch post offices every Thursday morning in front of the weekend, where the public cashed in their giros and pensions at the counter, even though The Mail pleaded with them to have the money transferred direct to their bank accounts. In London a lot of people didn't have bank accounts, even in this day and age. Besides, they liked to feel the crinkle of cash in the purse or pocket, so money was always flying around in big red armoured trucks. But armour is only as strong as its weakest part. And the weakest parts were always the humans inside the vehicles. Underpaid and often resentful, they were the links in the chain that parted easiest. But for once the human was more resentful of the robbers than his employers, and he paid dearly for his loyalty.

'It was only fucking money,' said Eddie, after the event. 'Just print some more. Anyway it wasn't his dough. Silly cunt.' The silly cunt in question being the driver's mate, a young man from Camden Town named Billy Liquorice.

The armoured van was driving down The Great West Road when three motors joined it. In front went first, a Ford Cosworth for the getaway driven by Robbo, a white Transit truck driven by Eddie, to block the road, with Joseph literally riding shotgun armed with an AK47, and behind, a Bedford tow truck to rip off the back doors with Connie at the wheel. All four had Tony Blair plastic masks hanging round their necks, and at the pre-arranged spot all four pulled them up over their faces. At nine ten precisely Eddie slammed on the brakes of the Transit and cut the Mail van off as Joseph jumped out and pointed the machine gun at the windscreen of the van. 'Switch off,' he screamed and fired a single shot at the engine compartment, as Connie spun the tow truck round in a tight circle. A woman in a Range Rover behind him tooted her horn, but at the sight of Tony Blair glaring back at her, and the sound of the shot she dived into the passenger well of the SUV and stayed there.

Now, if all had gone smoothly, the driver and his mate would have been forced out of the van as Eddie connected the tow-truck's hook to the handles on the back of the money wagon. But Billy Liquorice would have none of it. Even as the driver literally wet his trousers, Billy shoved him against the driver's door, got behind the wheel, slammed the van into reverse and drove back into the tow truck, then attempted to by-pass the Transit. The armoured vehicle slammed into the back of the trannie and stalled, and Joseph switched the AK to full automatic and fired through the passenger door of the van. The glass was supposed to be bullet proof, but the AK was loaded with armour piercing bullets and the side window imploded, covering Billy with shards of glass which almost cut his throat. He was lucky a bullet didn't blow his head off. So was Eddie, as he'd have been up for murder instead of the charges he faced. The tow truck had been pushed back into the bonnet of the Range Rover with enough force to ram the steering wheel back and inflate both air bags, narrowly missing the driver's face as she peered over the dashboard. Both radiators fractured sending clouds of steam into the morning air. When the gang heard sirens they abandoned the job, the trannie and the tow truck and made their escape, empty-handed in the Cosworth. The very next morning Eddie's lock up was raided, and the rest was history. As the evidence mounted, Sadie felt her spirits droop.

When day one was over, Sadie found Eddie whose bail had been retained, and they left by a side door where Tom had parked his car. But this time things were different. There was an imposing press and TV presence and Sadie and Eddie had to fight through a crowd of reporters shouting questions. They shielded themselves behind stony expressions and barged through the melee to the car, which screamed away with a shriek from its back tyres. 'Christ,' said Eddie. 'That was fucked.'

Tom kept his face to the front.

'I'm going down,' Eddie whispered in Sadie's ear. 'Things are looking bad.'

They drove the rest of the way home in silence, Sadie holding on to Eddie's hand as if she was drowning.

Once indoors Eddie said, 'Listen, I've spoken to my brief. I'm going to change my plea.'

'What?'

'It's all going pear shaped babe. I'm being let down by people I thought I could trust. If I cop a plea, then the judge might go a bit lightly.'

'But I thought everything was sorted? Like always?'

'I'm being fucked over darlin'.' Trust me, it's the only way. I promise you though, you'll be all right.'

But she wasn't.

The next day, Eddie did as he said and after the jury was excused, he was sentenced.

'This was a brutal and vicious robbery,' the judge

intoned. 'And although you have pleaded guilty, your accomplices are still at liberty, and you appear to show no remorse. I therefore sentence you to fifteen years in prison. Take him down.'

Sadie felt her world begin to slip away, and she almost fainted. Kate was on one side of her and Poppy the other with Niki sitting behind next to Connie. Sadie felt their hands supporting her and she knew she mustn't give in to the feelings of pure terror she was experiencing. Eddie would never forgive her the weakness, so she pulled herself together and left the court with her head held high.

She was allowed one brief interview with her husband in the holding cell in the bowels of the building. 'Sweetheart,' said Eddie. 'You'll be all right. When I'm settled we'll get you a VO.'

'Where are you going Eddie?' she asked

'The Marsh. I'll be close. Now don't worry. Love you.'

'Love you too,' said Sadie, and there wasn't much else to say.

17

Sadie hadn't been the only one to get a shock on the first day of the trial. At lunchtime Robbo, Joseph and Connie had gone off alone together. 'Business,' was all they said. 'See you later.'

'Looks like we're ladies who lunch alone then,' said Sadie to the other three girls. 'Eddie's brief told me there's a decent boozer round the corner. The Three Stags. Does a fair lunch. Though I'm not hungry, but I could go a livener. What about it?'

Poppy, Niki and Kate nodded agreement and they set off. Then Kate said,' Shit, I've run out of fags. I'll just nip in the shop.' Across the road was a newsagents.

'I've got plenty,' said Niki.

'Those things you smoke are too strong for me,' said Kate. 'Go on, I'll catch you up. Get me a G&T in.'

'Right,' said Sadie. 'He said it's left and left again. On the corner. Can't miss it.'

'Yeah. I'll look for three slags in the Three Stags,' said Kate, 'Then I'll know I'm there.'

'Cheek,' said Poppy, but they all laughed, grateful for the weak joke on a day where there wasn't much else to laugh about.

Kate trotted across the road and into the shop where she bought twenty Silk Cut purple. As she left and made to re-cross the road, a voice from the next doorway said, 'I hope you paid for those.'

Kate turned and there was Ali, standing there with a smile on his face.

Kate nearly fainted. He was the last person she wanted to see. Correction. The only person she wanted to see. But not under these circumstances. In a hotel bed with a bottle of champagne and a spliff he'd rolled to get them in the mood. So what the fuck was he doing outside the Old Bailey on the first day of Eddie's trial? 'What the hell are you doing here?' she demanded. 'If anyone sees us...'

'Everybody's off to lunch,' said Ali. 'I watched.'

'And I'm supposed to meet the girls.'

'You will. I'm not going to stop you. I just

wanted to say hello and that you look good enough to eat.'

'But what are you doing here?' Kate asked again.

'Wouldn't have missed it for the world. Seeing you lot together. One big happy family.'

'But you weren't in court... Were you?' she added.

'CCTV love. Smile, you're on candid camera. You do a lovely close-up.'

'Christ.'

'I had some time, and I wanted to see some of the trial. Not going well, is it?'

'Isn't it?'

'I'd say not. Teflon Eddie's in big trouble.'

'Don't ask me.'

'Anyhow, I'm off now. Things to do, people to see. Keep in touch.' And he smiled again, turned, walked off and vanished into the lunchtime crowds. Kate looked after him, and felt a pang that he was going.

She ran across the road, followed Sadie's directions and found the pub. 'You took your time,' said Poppy. 'Drink's getting warm.'

'Sorry, got lost,' said Kate. 'Who's got a light?'

As Ali walked away from Kate, it wasn't only her luscious body that was on his mind. He knew all about Eddie and the mail van robbery that had gone badly wrong, with three of the robbers still at large, and he knew who they were, but had no proof. Eddie led to Robbo and the other two cheap villains sitting up in the public gallery with their swag on their backs. Better suits that Ali could afford on his police salary. And with their flash birds, one of which at least would suck Ali's dick dry whenever he wanted. Kate. Ali yearned for her like a teenager with his first girlfriend. And there she was surrounded by the scum of east end villains. And he fucking envied them.

Bastards. Ali was no fool. He knew why he was on a fast track for promotion. The colour of his bloody skin. And he also knew people were watching him. Important people. Some ready to push him onwards and upwards, and others ready to drop him like a hot brick if he put a foot wrong. And shagging Kate Ellis wasn't a particularly good career move. Or maybe it was. Only time and results would tell. Besides, he couldn't leave her alone. She was like smack to a junkie. Catnip to his old mum's moggie. An addiction, and just spotting her there in court, and later in the street, was an aphrodisiac. But he kept a poker face, even though he saw hers go white at the sight of him. Keep calm, babe, he thought. Keep very calm.

Since Ali had first met Kate they'd managed to meet several times. Always at Kate's instigation. She called him on his mobile, gave a time she was free, and it was up to him to say yes or no. It had always been yes so far, even though he had to neglect his job sometimes to make the date. They always met at hotels where Ali booked the room, arrived first and waited for her in the bedroom. Their sex was sometimes fast and furious, sometimes tender and loving. Kate was the happiest she had been for years, but knew that if Robbo ever found out, she'd be in a world of pain.

Ali partly justified the meetings by any information he could glean about the gang during their pillow talk. Kate was wise to all that and gave little away, but Ali lived in hope. All he wanted to do was to get a lead on Robbo and the gang's plans, nick them, get them sent down and have Kate all to himself. That was his dream, but he knew that even if she was free, her background would always be suspect. But people in love, whatever ulterior motives they might have, constantly live in hope.

So when Eddie's trial came up, Ali wheedled his way into the court, on the pretext that when he moved up in rank, which he knew he would, he wanted to be *au fait* with all sorts of criminals. It was weak, but it worked. Ali sat in the CCTV control room and listened intently to the goings on. Later, when Eddie changed his plea, he thought, one down, three to go.

After lunch, as soon as there was a break, Kate made an excuse that she needed some air and left the building. As soon as she was clear, she found a bench in a tiny public park and called Ali. 'What the hell are do you think you're doing?' she demanded when he answered.

'This is not a good time cousin,' replied Ali. *Cousin* was part of their code.

'Bloody right it's not,' she hissed. 'I nearly fainted when I saw you.'

'Sorry, I couldn't let you know,' he replied. 'You know why.' He was still forbidden to call her.

'Christ,' she said. 'Are you going to be there again?'

'No. I've got a lot of other things to do. I was just in the area,' he lied.

'Thank Christ for that. When are we going to meet?'

'Up to you. Call me. I can't talk now, I'm with some senior officers and they're giving me the evil eye,' he whispered.

'I will,' and she hung up without a goodbye, and realised she was shaking. Fear, anger, lust, all mixed in a stew of emotion. She lit a cigarette and tried to relax, but stubbed it out half smoked, got up and went back to the court.

18

Kate had told no one about Ali. Not even Sadie, her best friend. She could just imagine the reaction. A copper, and an Asian to boot. Christ, that would set the cat amongst the pigeons. She suspected that Ali was grilling her about the workings of the gang, but she was convinced that wasn't what their affair was all about. He was too eager and loving to be that conniving. But she knew men, and their ways, so she was always careful.

The day after Eddie was sent down, Kate called Ali. 'Hello cousin,' he said. 'Long time.'

'I've been busy.'

'You're not the only one.'

'Yes. We need to meet.'

'When?'

'Tomorrow lunchtime?'

'Can do. The same place as last time?'

'Fine.'

'Call me tomorrow morning and I'll give you the details.'

'OK. I'll ring when I'm on my way. I should be there around one.'

'I'll be waiting.'

'We need to talk,' she said.

'And that's not all.'

'I'm serious.'

'So am I cousin, so am I.'

With that, and a quick goodbye, he broke the connection.

Their meeting place of choice was a Holiday Inn on the A12 close to the Millennium Dome, just south of the Blackwall tunnel. It was convenient with a big car park. Anonymous, but clean and safe, and the room service was discreet.

Kate phoned Ali *en route* and he gave her the room number. As usual he was first to arrive, and she took the lift to the fourth floor and tapped on the door. He welcomed her wearing a white towel wrapped round his waist, exposing his chocolate-coloured skin and taut stomach. His hair was wet and shiny, and she thought he looked good enough to eat. 'Thought I'd take a shower,' he said.

'Be nice and clean for you.'

'Are you working?' she asked as she closed the door behind her and he swept her up in his arms.

'Supposed to be. Just routine enquiries. My time's my own.'

'Lucky you.'

He smiled. 'Lunch? I've ordered us chicken salads and coffee as we're both driving.'

'Aren't you law abiding?' she said.

'Neither of us needs a pull at this time, right?'

She nodded agreement.

They were interrupted by a knock on the door and lunch was served. Ali gave the waitress a tip and she left.

'You wanted to talk,' he said. 'Let's do it over lunch, then get down to the important things in life—us, and sex.'

She smiled. Ali could always charm her round his little finger. They sat together at the table over-looking the busy road outside and tucked in. 'So, what's up?' said Ali round a mouthful of food.

'You, turning up at the court, that's what.'

'I'm a copper. That's my job.'

'Not Eddie's case.'

'So what?' he asked again. 'He got what he deserved.'

'Maybe.'

'Connie, Robbo and Joseph were the others on

the blag weren't they?' he asked innocently.

'As if I'd tell you if they were.'

'No. The old code, right?' he said sarcastically.

'It was how I was brought up.'

'Which is why you never told about what your father did to you and your mother. Or what Robbo does to you now.'

She looked away, the food turning sour in her mouth. 'That's none of your business.'

'It is Kate,' he insisted, 'I think I love you, and it hurts me to see what you have to go through.' Kate was shocked at his revelation. Shocked and excited, but tried to stay cool.

'Not half as much as it hurts me,' she said. 'And you only think. What good is that?'

'Christ Kate, give me a break.'

'Typical man. Wants his cake and eat it too.'

'So tell me, how do you feel about me?'

'Me. Always me. Like I said, a typical man.'

'So what are you saying? Is this it? Did you come down today to give me the elbow?'

She threw the remains of her food down onto her plate. 'I can't. I can't give you up, whatever happens. But I know it's so wrong. Robbo would kill you, then me, if he ever found out. I could never forgive myself if something happened to you.'

'Christ, but you had me worried there. I mean it

Kate. About loving you I mean. But I was scared to own up. What with everything that's going on. I'm putting my life in your hands, you know that.'

'I know.'

'So tell me something,' he pleaded. 'Anything. I don't do this. Beg, I mean.'

'Doesn't go with your self-image, tough guy?'

'You could say that, but right now I don't care.'

'Good.' She smiled.

'So you do have feelings for me?'

'Of course I do.'

'Then let's go to bed,' he said. 'I'm not hungry anymore. At least, not for food.'

So they did.

The sex was wonderful as always. Ali seemed even more passionate with their every meeting, and Kate gladly gave herself up to him, coming time and time again until she was exhausted. But she couldn't shake off the feeling that Ali was more interested in what her husband and the remainder of the gang were doing, than her. Paranoia, she thought as he reached for her again. It has to be. But she was wrong.

19

The weeks passed since Eddie's imprisonment, things went from bad to worse for Sadie. All her married life, she'd been protected from reality by her husband. He came home with the dough, and she spent it. End of. He'd choose their houses, cars, and other major purchases. Sure, Sadie had a say in them, but as soon as they'd made a joint decision, the money arrived, and all was taken care of. Eddie paid the bills too. Credit cards, mortgage, utilities were all in his name, and he dealt with them. Now it was Sadie's job, and pretty quickly she discovered that they were in deep financial difficulties. Every day bills printed in red dropped through the letterbox. And worse, she started getting increas-

ingly stern phone calls from various financial insti-
tutions, demanding prompt payment for debts she
didn't even know they had.

She checked their bank accounts and found that
what she had once thought of as bottomless pits,
were pretty well all empty. They owed the building
society. The cars she thought were theirs were
leased, and the payments well in arrears. Even her
precious gold card was up to and beyond its limit,
and she couldn't even afford to pay the minimum
payment each month. Worse than the red bank bills
were the threatening calls from loan sharks who
would stop at nothing to get back their money,
with interest. Sadie knew it would only be a matter
of time before one of them got his goons to pay her
a house call, safe now Eddie was away.

The next time she received a visiting order she
went along to the prison with her handbag full of
final demands.

She sat in the cheerless visitor's room as Eddie
came in. 'Hello doll,' he said. 'You OK?'

'No Eddie, I'm not,' she replied, avoiding contact
as he tried to touch her hand. 'What the fuck has
been going on?'

'Not guilty,' he replied. 'I'm inside, remember?'

'How can I forget? Every day I get reminders.
Final ones mostly.'

'What?'

'Bills, Eddie. Great big fucking bills—everything from the phones to the council tax. What happened?'

'Shit happened love. I got stitched up and chucked in here.'

'But there was that forty grand…'

'Every penny gone. Briefs who screwed up. Bent cops who took the shilling then got a conscience. A judge who retired early on medical grounds and who's living in bloody Portugal in a villa I bought. It's endless darlin'.'

'So are these debts Eddie.'

'What can I say love? What can I do?'

'Aren't you owed?'

'Yeah. Plenty. But there's nothing I can do from inside the shovel.'

'What about the other boys?'

Eddie pulled a regretful face. 'They helped out. I owe them too if the truth be known. Don't worry. They won't be coming round for their dough. They know the situation.'

'What about the bank deposit boxes? You've still got them haven't you?'

'Sure. But believe me, they're not stuffed with cash. You'd know if they were.'

'So what is in them?'

He hesitated. 'OK sweetheart. I'll tell you. But not a word.'

'Go on then,' she said.

He hardly moved his lips as he spoke. Nobody knew who might be watching. 'There's shooters, ammo, and the plans for a big job,' he said. 'I was going to tell you in time.'

'Thanks for keeping me in the loop.'

'Sorry. Listen, I'll speak to Lewis at the solicitors. He's got the keys. He doesn't know which banks or the numbers. He's got a letter for you with all the details inside. It's sealed. Make sure it still is when you get it. I'll put in a call today. You got tomorrow. The boys are going to do the job. I'm the architect as always. You'll get a cut. Otherwise, you'll have to duck and dive Sade. Do what you can. I'm fucked in here.'

'Not literally I hope.'

'No love. There's prettier fish than me to fry. Thank God for that. Anyway, I can take care of myself. Always have. I'm just extra careful about dropping the soap in the shower. Know what I mean?' And he laughed.

Sadie didn't share the joke. 'I miss you Eddie,' she said, and meant it.

'I miss you too doll. I wish I was out there with you. Us against the world, remember?'

'Course I do.'

'Right. You get busy. See Lewis, then see the chaps. You'll be OK, I swear.'

So be it, she thought. I'm on my own now. It's all down to me. No more leaning on men who screw you seven ways from Sunday. Fuck the lot of them. I'm on my own, and I'm tougher than any of them. I'll have to be. But deep down inside she was as nervous as a kitten. So she hardened her heart, straightened her spine and moved on.

20

---✦-◆-✦---

Sadie did just as Eddie told her to. She rang Jack
Lewis at the local solicitor they used for small jobs.
Not criminal work. He was a pleasant bloke in his
mid forties, and he told Sadie he was free from
noon onwards. She arrived bang on time and was
shown into his office where he offered her coffee
which she accepted. He ushered her to a seat, and
offered his condolences for Eddie's state.

'He's not dead,' she said.

'I know Mrs Ross. My apologies. I didn't mean it
quite like that.'

'Sorry,' she said. 'I'm just a bit touchy these
days.'

'I quite understand.'

They were interrupted by his assistant bringing in their refreshments, and when they were settled, he said. 'I had a call from Mr Ross yesterday from... er, well, you know where. I have certain items in my possession he wishes to pass on to you.'

'Any money?' she asked hopefully.

'I'm sorry, no. At least, not that I'm aware. A sealed letter and some keys. There could be some money in the envelope, but from the size of it, I doubt it.' He opened a drawer in his desk and pulled out a large brown envelope which he emptied on to his blotter. There were three keys on a ring, each marked with a white sticker. On the stickers were the numbers, 1,2,3. There was also a thin white envelope, taped around the edges and sealed with a blob of red wax. 'That's it I'm afraid,' said Lewis. 'If you'll just sign a receipt it's all yours. And if there's anything else I can do...'

Sadie put down her cup on the edge of the desk. 'Thank you,' she said. 'You've always been very kind to us. Do I owe you anything?'

He smiled. 'No Mrs Ross. We're all up to date.' He passed her over a receipt book which she signed. She then rose to leave as he handed her the brown envelope in which he had replaced the keys and letter. 'As I said,' he continued. 'Anything the firm can do, just get in touch.'

'I will,' said Sadie, who made her farewells and left.

She opened the letter in the car. It was a short, typed note. Just the names of three local banks, one which she could see from where she was sitting, numbers of the safety deposit accounts, passwords, and which of the three keys she'd need to open each. She took the key for the bank across the road, along with the letter, and went to see what exactly it was that Eddie had hidden so carefully.

It was easy. She asked to see a manager at the cash window, told him the number and password, and he did the rest. She was shown downstairs to the safety deposit room. He had a duplicate key, they both turned theirs in the locks, and when he tugged the drawer out of its slot, she was left alone in a small room with the box. It was heavy, and when she opened it she knew why. Inside were three handguns that looked brand new, neatly boxed, illustrated, and trade marked GLOCK 19. Inside each of the boxes was a little booklet. Underneath them, was what she recognised from all the gangster movies she and Eddie had watched together, as a machine pistol. An Uzi. She left two of the pistols inside the box, putting the third in her handbag along with the booklet. She was amazed how light it was. Nothing like she'd imagined. More like a toy than a real gun. But if Eddie had obtained them, she knew they'd be real enough. She relocked the safety deposit box, had it returned to its home and left.

Inside the next bank she found the ammunition. Hundreds of brass jacketed rounds, slotted into the kind of thick white foam that previously she'd only seen protecting domestic items in their packaging. Each box contained fifty bullets. The boxes were all marked 9 MILLIMETRE, with the name of the manufacturer from some Middle American state. At the bottom of the box were four ammunition magazines. Three were short and looked like they fitted the Glock hidden in her bag. The fourth was longer, and she guessed that one belonged to the Uzi. She took a box of fifty rounds and put them in her bag too. She realised with all that she'd found she could start a small war, and maybe that's what she would have to do to get out of trouble.

Bring it on, she thought.

Inside the third bank she discovered the plan Eddie had told her about. It was printed out on A4 paper and neatly bound in clear plastic. Trust him, she thought. If he hadn't turned to a life of crime he might have been a good pen-pusher.

When she left the bank the folder was under her arm, and the deposit drawer was empty.

She went back home, made herself a drink and sat down to read the book. But before she did, with the help of the instruction manual she worked out how to load the Glock's magazine, although it cost her a slice out of one of her fingers, and how to work the trigger mounted safety catch. She loaded a shell in the chamber and put the gun, which was a lot heavier when loaded, on the table next to the sofa where she sat, feeling pleased with herself.

21

Whilst Sadie and Kate were otherwise engaged, Poppy and Niki had become firm friends. Previously, they'd never really chatted without Sadie and Kate being there, but a mutual addiction to nicotine had thrown them together often outside the Bailey whilst Eddie's brief trial had been going on inside.

They had agreed to meet afterwards, even though Niki assumed Connie would object, and told Poppy so. But Eddie's incarceration seemed to be weighing on his mind, and he just dismissed her with a grunted 'whatever' when she told him, which she took for a yes.

The two women's homes were equal distance

from Canary Wharf, so they started to get together there and spend their days window-shopping. Poppy spent Joseph's money prolifically, and couldn't understand why Niki was on such a tight budget. 'Connie doesn't like me having my own money,' Niki explained on their second meeting over coffee in one of the many little restaurants inside the wharf.

'Why not?' asked Poppy.

Niki shrugged, a uniquely Russian shrug that said a lot without words. 'He's worried I might run away I suppose. He bought and paid for me.'

'That's disgusting. It would serve him right if you did, tight arse.'

Niki laughed. 'Tight arse,' she said. 'I like that.'

'Joe doesn't care what I spend,' said Poppy. 'Doesn't care much about what I do these days.'

'Why not?'

Poppy told Niki about her impossibility of conceiving and about Joseph's baby mother and child.

'And you put up with it?' asked Niki.

'You put up with Connie.'

'I suppose so.'

'I'd like to kill that bitch, and her bastard, and Joseph for that matter,' said Poppy, the bitterness inside her spilling out like bile.

'And I dream of Connie being dead,' said Niki.

'A life of my own…'

'But it'll never happen,' said Poppy.

'I could kill Joseph,' said Niki.

'You,' said Poppy, laughing. 'You're just a little slip of a girl. I've seen Joe take three or four men on. And win.'

It was Niki's turn to laugh as she shared her story of the three thugs she'd taken on in Millwall Park.'

'You're kidding,' said Poppy. 'You do martial arts?'

'My daddy and grandpapa taught me well. They were soldiers. Russian soldiers. The best in the world. Cossacks. Wild men. Grandpapa was at Stalingrad. You know about Stalingrad?'

Poppy shook her head.

'It was a famous battle in the Second World War.'

'I didn't go to school much,' said Poppy. 'I'm ashamed about the things I don't know. Tell me.'

Niki explained about the long, cold battle for the city, that defeated Hitler's mighty army, and helped win the Second World War for the allies.

'They were starving,' said Niki. 'Inside the city. They ate the dead when the rations ran out. Can you imagine that?'

Poppy shook her head in disgust.

'But my grandpapa killed a hundred Germans. He was a shooter. A sniper. He taught me to use weapons. But he also taught me to kill silently using just my hands and feet.'

'Christ,' said Poppy. 'Have you ever killed anyone?'

Niki smiled. 'None of your business.'

'You have. Jesus.'

'Jesus had nothing to do with it.'

'So tell me.'

'Two men tried to rape me,' said Niki. 'Back home. I was sixteen. They drove the roads where I lived, and found women alone. Any woman, any age. It was a famous case, but the police were useless.'

'Most police are,' said Poppy.

Niki nodded agreement. 'One afternoon I was walking home from school, when they found me. They were strong. They hit me from behind and I woke up in the back of their car. I heard them talking, and knew they were the men who had been doing those terrible things.'

'Weren't you scared?' asked Poppy.

'Terrified. But I knew terror was... How do you say it. Not productive.'

Poppy nodded, engrossed in the story.

'They drove into the woods near my home. It is a terrible place. Dark and cold. No one goes there. It's like a forest in a fairy story where the bad fairies live.'

Poppy was mesmerised.

'They dragged me out of the car, and one held me down whilst the other dropped his pants. He pushed up my skirt, and was going to pull down my underwear when I kicked him in his balls. He screamed like a girl, and the other one let me go and pulled out a knife. I didn't tell you, but the other women were all stabbed and killed. Stabbed in their privates. A terrible thing.'

Poppy remained silent as the business of the Wharf went on around them.

'I like knives,' said Niki. 'Grandad had a collection. I took the knife off the man easily. You see he couldn't believe a young girl in school uniform could hurt him. He must have though the kick I gave his friend was just luck. Anyway, I took the knife out of his hand like taking a lollipop from a child. Then I stabbed him. In the heart. He was dead as he fell.'

'What about his friend?' Poppy could hardly catch her breath.

'I cut off his cock and put it in his mouth. I left them both there and walked home. It wasn't far. Months later some woodcutters found them. It was in the papers.'

'What about the knife?' asked Poppy.

'It's at home,' said Niki. 'I brought it with me from Russia. I smuggled it here, and one day I will cut Connie's cock off too and stuff it in his mouth, just like that bastard who tried to rape me. Do you want me to go?'

'Why?' asked Poppy.

'Because.'

'No love,' interrupted Poppy. 'I feel safer with you around.'

22

The plan that Eddie had prepared was a blueprint for the perfect crime. That night, as Sadie sat in her lonely house, the only light came from an angle-poise lamp next to her, illuminating the dull sheen of the loaded pistol on the table below. She read the book twice. Once, quickly, to get the gist of the robbery, and then again slowly, absorbing all the details.

The plan was simple: Every month, regular as clockwork, an armoured truck left the headquarters of one of the major banks stuffed with worn out bank notes due to be incinerated at a furnace in Kent. Well, not quite clockwork. More as irregular as a Rolex manufactured in Taiwan. The cargo went on different days of the month. Different times. Different routes. Even different amounts of money. Sometimes as much as thirty-million quid, sometimes as little as ten. But one thing was certain. The notes had to be destroyed as they simply took up too much room at the bank. And nothing else but burning would do. That was the Treasury rules. No shredding, no pulping. The money, and more importantly, the special paper it was printed on, had to be destroyed. The first problem for anyone wanting to have a pop at this prize was finding out how much was going to be on board. If an attempt at a hijack was going to be made, it had better be a bumper bundle. Next, when exactly that particular truck was going to be on the move. They were all identical. Based on the chassis of a long wheel base Ford Transit, the bodies were steel lined, and the driver and his mate had no way of opening the rear doors. The third problem was the crew. That was vital, because Eddie needed someone on board who could be forced, by hook or by crook to work with the gang. Someone with a family, who Eddie intended to take hostage on the day of the robbery. Very risky. But it had been done before. The fourth was the actual route. And finally, what to do with a truckload of filthy dirty cash once you'd got hold of it. Even though the notes were thin and worn, that much cash wouldn't go into a suitcase.

Eddie had the answers to all of these dilemmas. Somehow, he'd got an inside man. He called him Deep Throat, after the Watergate whistle blower. Sadie had no idea Eddie had such a sense of humour. No actual name for the inside man was mentioned. Sadie guessed that by coercion, bribery, threat, or possibly all three, Eddie could find out the details of the drop. Next, a friend of a friend as Eddie called him, once again nameless, would take the cash at fifty pence to the pound no questions asked, with transport to be supplied by the purchaser.

There were just a few other snags. All the bank's trucks were fitted with the latest state-of-the-art satellite tracking system, and of course sophisticated communication between the vehicle and base. So anyone on the rob had to get inside the thing and disable all comms. That was why Eddie needed an unwilling accomplice on board.

Blimey, thought Sadie, not easy. But quite a coup if someone could get away with it.

The actual rip off was simplicity itself. When the route was known, which would be the day before, two JCB heavy-duty mobile earth moving shovels would trap the money truck front and back, the crew would be removed from the vehicle and one JCB would smash open the rear doors. The money that had been counted and bagged up at the bank, then put into cages would be removed and transferred to the gang's truck, the JCB's would be torched on site, and everyone would be a great deal richer.

End of story.

It was an audacious plan. If it worked it would net a lot of money, and if it failed... Well, nothing was perfect.

Sadie put down the book that Eddie had so carefully prepared. It was a four man job, and Sadie knew exactly who would be involved. But who would be the fourth man, now Eddie was banged up tight?

Right chaps, she thought. Time for a meet I think.

The next day she got in touch with Connie and told him they needed to get together, but gave no details.

He grudgingly agreed, as if Sadie was on the borrow, which in a way she was. She wanted the robbery to go ahead, succeed, and get Eddie's cut as the architect.

But first she wanted to test out the gun she'd taken from the safety deposit at the bank. She didn't know when she might need it.

23

The next morning, after a breakfast of bio-yoghurt, muesli with strawberries and coffee, Sadie loaded the other magazine she'd taken from the second bank deposit drawer with its fifteen 9mm bullets. Retrieving the already loaded Glock from its hiding place, she wrapped both guns in an old sweater and stashed them under the spare wheel in her 4WD Mercedes.

She drove down to Epping, into the forest where she and Eddie had done some courting, which was a euphemism for some hot and heavy sex in the back of the Jaguar he'd owned at the time. She drove off road until she was deep in the woods, far away, she hoped from prying eyes and ears.

She opened the back of her SUV and took out the gun and spare ammunition clip. Just holding it turned her insides to water. It was all very well reading the instructions, but she had never held a gun in her life before, and although it was a light-weight piece, it still felt hot and heavy in her trembling, sweaty hands.

She looked round for a target. There was a lightning struck tree about fifteen metres away, its blackened trunk strangely looking like the shape of a man, and it would do.

Here goes, she thought gripping the pistol in both hands like they did in the films, and she squeezed the safety, and pulled the trigger. The noise of the shot seemed massive in the quiet woods, and the gun kicked, and she almost dropped the thing as the bullet went God knows where.

'Fuck,' she said aloud, in a voice she hardly recognised through the ringing in her ears. 'That was no bloody good.'

She relaxed her grip slightly and fired again, and a strip of wood sprang from the very edge of the tree. She smiled and fired again, then once more, as she grew more confident. When the gun was empty she went and looked at the trunk of the tree. She counted eight hits out of the fifteen rounds she'd fired, and thought that was pretty good for a beginner. She dropped out the empty magazine, inserted the spare, slapped it home, depressed the lever at the side, and the action clicked home. She put a bullet in the chamber, but decided she'd been in the clearing too long, and made enough noise to wake the dead, so it was time to split. She stored the Glock and the empty magazine away again and drove home. She saw no one, coming or going.

She'd arranged to meet Connie that afternoon, and arrived on time at his house on the Island. He was alone. 'Niki's out with her mate Poppy,' he growled. 'Those two are always together these days.'

'You don't approve?' asked Sadie.

'Couldn't give a fuck really,' Connie replied. 'As long as she's home in time to make my tea.'

Nice, thought Sadie. 'Look Connie I'll come straight to the point. Eddie's told me about this job you lot are going to do.'

'What job?' Connie interrupted

'The bank truck. Old cash.'

'Don't know what you're talking about.'

'I think you do.'

'Not women's business.'

'It's this woman's business. I'm skint, Connie. Going under. I need money.'

Connie shrugged. 'You've had a pot, the pair of

you over the years. If it's all gone it's not my problem.'

Sadie could hardly believe her ears. 'What's the matter with you Connie?' Sadie demanded. 'You're mates. The old firm.'

'Eddie's away. The old firm don't exist no more.'

'And if he'd talked to the law, so would you be.'

'He'll be looked after.'

'So you do know about the job?'

'Maybe.'

'And?'

'And we'll do it, when we're ready.'

'When Deep Throat gives you the word.'

'Deep Throat,' Connie mocked. 'Whose bright idea was that?'

'Do you know who he is?'

'Course I do.'

'Who?'

He touched the side of his nose. 'What you don't know can't hurt you.'

'And what will Eddie's cut be?'

'Whatever we give him. He always was too flash, your Eddie.'

Sadie felt like getting the gun she had in her car and putting one in Connie's head, but she kept calm. 'What happens when I tell Eddie what you've said?'

'Tell him. See if I care. We'll do the bizzo when

we're good and ready, and you'll get what's his. What's the fucking problem?'

'I don't like your attitude.'

'Get over it.'

'I never thought it would come to this Connie.'

'But it has. Now if that's all, I've got things to do.'

Sadie left the house and sat in her car looking at Connie's front door. 'Right,' she said aloud. 'If that's the way it's going to be. Bring it on.'

24

Eddie gave Sadie a ring most days when his phone card was in credit. She'd already told him she'd done what he'd told her at her last visit, without giving any details. Walls have ears, and so do pay phones in the nick. 'Gotta see you,' she said. 'Urgent.'

'What's rattled your cage?' he asked.

'I'll tell you when I see you.'

'OK, I'll get a VO sorted,' he said. 'You're OK though?'

'I'm all right, it's the rest of the world's what's fucked.'

'See you soon,' he said, and hung up.

She got a visitor's order for the day after next,

and could hardly contain her impatience as she remembered Connie's attitude, and the bills kept piling up.

She was first in line for the visit, and when Eddie joined her at the table, he said, 'Where's the fire?'

'Listen,' she said in a stage whisper. 'Your mates have gone off the reservation.'

'Not so fast,' he interrupted. 'You checked the boxes?'

'Yes. I told you.'

'Everything I said. Was there, I mean.'

'Yeah.'

'So, go see the boys and tell them you speak on my behalf.'

'I already did.'

'That was quick. Who?' he asked.

'Connie.'

Eddie nodded approval. 'And?'

'More or less told me to fuck off.'

'You know Connie,' said Eddie. 'He's old school. Don't believe that women should be in the loop.'

'Eddie,' said Sadie. 'He said the old firm's dead and buried. You're in here. They're going to do the job and throw a few crumbs our way.'

'I bet he never meant that. You got the wrong end of the stick.'

'Did I bollocks. He had me out of the house so fast my bum nearly caught fire.'

'Sounds like Connie.'

'What? Is that it? Sounds like fucking Connie. Are you having a laugh?'

'Keep your voice down, love,' said Eddie. 'You'll frighten the screws.'

'Christ,' Said Sadie. 'I expected more than this from you. Are you going stir soft?'

Eddie shrugged. 'What can I say?'

'You can say that little bastard did the mail van with you, and end up sharing a cell.'

'Can't do it love. It's against the code.'

'Fuck the code.'

'I don't grass,' said Eddie. 'Whatever happens.'

'So what about me? Does he know everyone involved? The real names?'

Eddie nodded. 'We had to keep on top of things. In touch. Soon as I knew I was in for a stretch, I told Connie and the boys the lot.'

'Jesus,' said Sadie. 'No wonder he told me to take a hike. He can drop you right out. Honour amongst thieves eh?'

'This thief.'

'But Eddie, what am I going to do? We're going to lose the house, the cars, everything.'

'Start again doll.'

'What? And you expect me to be there when you get out? Seven years and change if you're a good boy. Otherwise, when?'

'I'm sorry love. You could always get a job you know. Flog the place off. We've got equity. Buy a flat.'

'Christ Eddie. What's happened to you? This isn't the man I married.'

'It's the man you're married to now. I done all right by you girl. Now go and sort something out for yourself.'

'I don't believe this,' said Sadie.

'Listen love. I know what you got up to when I was out and about at work. You shagging anything with a dick. I never done nothing because I was at it myself. You pissed on our marriage with those geezers. Now you're on your own. And I warn you, there's worse to come.'

'You bastard,' Sadie almost spat.

Eddie shrugged, and with tears in her eyes Sadie got up and left the room, without another word or a backward glance.

25

---✦---

By this time Poppy and Niki were lovers, their friendship gradually having evolved into something deeper. It started in the changing room of one of the boutiques on Canary Wharf. The two women had met for morning coffee, as had become a habit. They enjoyed their freedom and each other's company, as the hordes of office workers and construction workers swarmed through the place. 'Think it'll ever be finished?' asked Poppy, as yet another bunch of builders in overalls and hard hats passed by, clutching bags from one or other of the sandwich shops that fed them.

'What, this place?' said Niki. 'I don't know. Seems that every time a new tower is finished, they start on another. I can see them from my bedroom window. It's like on the Island. All they do is build more flats on every available space. I think if you left a car in the street for long enough someone would try to put a penthouse on top of it.'

They both laughed, and Poppy bit into one of the pastries they'd bought. 'How come you speak such good English?' asked Poppy. 'You're amazing for someone who hasn't been here long.'

'American films at home in Russia. On satellite and video. And I had a good language teacher at school. I'm lousy at mathematics though.'

Poppy laughed. 'I'm lousy at everything. Fancy a go round the shops?' she asked.

'Sure.'

They wandered through the malls, stopping every now and again to admire a garment or a pair of shoes, or sometimes to wonder who would be seen dead in something or other.

Then Niki saw a dress she loved. It was nothing special. Nothing flash. Just basic black that even Connie couldn't moan about. But if course she had no money or card to buy it with.

'Try it on,' said Poppy. 'Can't hurt. If it looks good I'll treat you.'

'I can't,' said Niki. 'It's too much.'

'It's Joe's money,' sad Poppy. 'And if I spend

some on you, at least the bitch and her bastard won't get it.'

They went inside. The shop was empty apart from a blonde behind the counter studying *Heat* magazine and filing a nail. 'The dress in the window,' said Poppy. 'Black. Have you got a size...?' She looked at Niki.

'Eight,' she said.

'Lucky girl,' said the assistant. 'I can't get below a ten whatever I do. Let's have a look.'

She went over to a rail and swished through the dresses on it, until she pulled one out. 'An eight it is. They come up a bit small I warn you, but I think it should be fine with your figure. Give it a try. Dressing room's through there.' She handed Niki the dress and pointed to a narrow corridor between more racks of clothes, and went back to her magazine.

Niki took the dress and followed the assistant's directions. Poppy wandered round the shop picking things up and putting them back.

'Poppy,' Niki called from the back. 'Come see.'

Poppy did as she was bid, and followed the sound of Niki's voice into a miniscule, curtained closet. The dress fitted Niki's slim frame perfectly. Her tiny breasts stood out, the nipples visible through the thin fabric, and the skirt finished just above her bare knees. 'Fabulous,' said Poppy, experiencing a strange feeling as she stood close enough to Niki to feel her breath. 'You've got to have it.'

'Thank you Poppy,' said Niki, throwing her arms around her friend, and kissing her full on the mouth. Their lips parted and their tongues touched, and for the first time in her life Poppy gave another woman a kiss on the lips.

'Did you like that?' asked Niki when they pulled apart.

Poppy nodded, too breathless to answer.

'I thought you would.'

'Everything OK in there?' called the assistant.

'Yes, coming,' stuttered Poppy.

'Now let me get dressed and let's get out of here,' said Niki, mischievously.

Poppy paid for the dress on her card and the two women stood outside the shop. Poppy had never felt such a rush of desire. Not with Joseph or anyone before. 'What shall we do?' she asked.

'There's a hotel around the corner. We could go there,' said Niki.

And like a pair of teenage girls, they ran off laughing towards the Four Seasons hotel.

26

They got a room easily. Poppy gave her card details, and no one turned a hair at their lack of luggage apart from the bag from the boutique. She took a suite on the top floor with a breathtaking view over central London to one side, and Greenwich and Blackheath on the other, with the iron-grey Thames snaking beneath them. 'It's fabulous,' said Niki as she went out onto the balcony. 'Look, you can see my house. It's tiny. If Connie came out into the garden, and I had a sniper's rifle, he wouldn't know what hit him.'

Poppy didn't know what had hit her either. She suddenly panicked, and Niki, looking back through the window knew it. 'Come out here

Poppy,' she said. 'Have a smoke. Relax.'

'I don't...'

'I know. But you will.'

Poppy joined Niki on the balcony. The world seemed to swim beneath her from the great height, and she reached for her friend for support. They stood there holding each other as they shared a cigarette. 'I've never done anything like this before,' said Poppy.

'Nor had I until I did,' said Niki. 'At school.'

'Seems to me you had a pretty colourful school career,' said Poppy. 'Mind you, so did I. I got pregnant. That's why I can't...'

'I know. I know, my darling Poppy,' said Niki.

They finished the cigarette and Niki flipped it over the balcony rail, and they watched it fall, pulled by the breeze until it was out of sight, lost in the waters of the river.

They went back inside and Niki found the mini bar. 'Champagne,' she said.

'Might as well be hung for a sheep as a lamb,' said Poppy.

'A strange expression,' said Niki. 'Sheep, lambs. That's us. You won't get into trouble will you. For spending all this money, I mean.'

'No. Joe's very careful not to stir things up too much these days. He doesn't care anyway.'

'Then let's enjoy it,' said Niki. She went though

into the bedroom and exclaimed. 'Just look at the size of this bed. And the bathroom. It's beautiful.'

Poppy was pleased with her friend's excitement and followed. Niki was just in her briefs again, her coat and dress slung over a chair. 'You're beautiful,' said Poppy.

'So are you Poppy,' said Niki. 'You don't know how beautiful. Now come to bed.'

Shyly, Poppy stripped off her outer clothes, then her bra. 'Your breasts are beautiful,' said Niki. 'I've never known a black woman before.'

'Half-black,' Poppy corrected her. 'By my dad.'

'He must've been a handsome man, and your mother as gorgeous as you.'

'Once,' said Poppy, thinking of the shrunken woman in her tiny flat, which could also probably be seen from the eyrie where they now were. 'Once.'

They both got into bed and toasted each other with their champagne flutes. 'Are you happy?' asked Niki.

'For the first time in ages,' said Poppy.

They laid their glasses on the matching bedside cabinets and they hugged. Niki took the initiative and kissed Poppy's mouth again, a long, lingering kiss that seemed to last forever. When they parted Poppy said, 'That was wonderful.'

Niki slid her hands to her breasts and gently

stroked them before taking one nipple in her mouth, her dark hair covering Poppy's tummy. 'That's even better,' breathed Poppy, taking one of Niki's tits in her hand too. 'Don't stop.'

Barely a moment later Poppy lay back on the white sheets, trembling. 'I've never come that fast,' she whispered.

'Let's have another drink,' said Niki. 'Then you can do me. Let's see how fast I can come too.'

27

Niki looked down at Poppy as she lay recovering from the strongest orgasm she'd ever known. Poppy couldn't believe how the young Russian girl had made her feel, and couldn't wait to reciprocate, but she was exhausted. 'I need a drink first,' she said. 'And a cigarette.'

'Are you being cruel to me?' asked Niki. 'Making me wait?'

'No love,' said Poppy, reaching for her hand and giving it a squeeze. 'I'm just... God, I don't know what I am. Give me a minute will you.'

'Take as long as you want,' said Niki. 'There's no rush is there?'

'No. Joseph's out with the bitch and the brat as

usual. What about you?'

'As long as Connie's tea, as he calls it, is ready for six o'clock, then he doesn't care. He thinks I'm safe with you.'

'And you are darling,' said Poppy, sipping at her champagne, and sitting up in bed to light a ciga- rette. 'And we've got hours.'

Hours that they spent exploring each other.

When they were lying close together under a sheet, when Niki had tumbled off her, Poppy asked, 'What did you say?'

'When?'

'When you were all excited. Russian wasn't it?'

'Yes. I just said that I loved you and wanted you forever.'

'Forever is a long time.'

'I know. And I know things can't go on like this, now we're…'

'What?'

'Lovers. Together. That's what you want isn't it?'

'Yes.'

'Be sure. We're playing a dangerous game.'

'I am sure. And I know we're playing with fire, but I don't care,' Poppy said tenderly, looking into Niki's eyes.

'We must be careful. You know what Connie's like.'

'We will be.'

'I know we will. Do you want to come again my sweet?' asked Niki.

'Again and again, and again.'

'Then you shall. Do you ever use things?'

'What things?'

'Sex toys. Dildos, vibrators?'

'I used to. My mates bought me one of those Rampant Rabbits from Ann Summers for my birthday,' said Poppy, blushing. 'How about you?'

'What is a rampant rabbit?' Niki looked quizzical, and Poppy thought she would burst out laughing as she explained. 'I don't have anything like that. Connie would go crazy. But I do use this.' She hopped out of bed and found her handbag, from which she pulled out her mobile phone and switched it on. She fiddled with the controls whilst Poppy poured more champagne for them both.

'What are you doing?' asked Poppy. 'Who are you calling? Not Connie?'

'Don't be crazy. There.' And Niki pushed a button and the phone started buzzing in her hand. 'I've put it on to vibrate. Now open your legs.'

'Niki, you're terrible,' said Poppy, and laughed out loud.

The early afternoon sped past, and soon it was time for them to part. 'I'll never forget today,' said Poppy as she repaired her make up and got dressed. 'As long as I live. We will do it again, won't we?'

'Of course. Whenever you want. Whenever we can.'

'Soon?'

'As soon as is possible, but the men must never guess. Not until we're ready.'

'Ready for what?'

'To kill them, what else?' said Niki, coldly.

'Are you kidding?'

'Never been more serious in my life.'

Poppy could hardly believe her ears. 'Christ, that's a bit strong. We can't.'

'Then we'll be on the run for the rest of our lives.'

'Better that than murdering our husbands!'

'Poppy, you don't get it. This is the most serious thing either of us will ever do. If we're together, we go all the way.'

'Or what?'

'Or we cannot be together.'

'Oh Niki, you'll have to be strong enough for both of us.'

'For you Poppy, I'll be strong enough for an army.'

'I love you,' said Poppy.

'I love you too.'

'Then I'll do it.'

'I never had any doubts.'

And they kissed again.

28

By this time Sadie was almost at her wit's end. There was no cash in the coffers, and she was reduced to pawning some jewellery just to survive. And worse. Eddie's most hurtful betrayal came when she returned from visiting him at the prison, to find a 'For Sale' sign outside the house. She phoned the number on the board and spoke to a rather disinterested woman, who told her that Jack Lewis had organised the transaction. 'We'll need to get in,' the woman said. 'To look around. Appraise the value of the property.'

'Over my fucking dead body,' said Sadie, and slammed down the phone. Only to pick it up again and call the solicitor. 'What's going on Jack?' she demanded, almost in tears. 'My bloody house is being sold out from under me.'

'And you were unaware?'

'Of course I bloody well was. Why do you think I'm phoning you now?'

'As a matter of fact I've been trying to get in touch with you on the same subject.'

'My mobile's dead,' said Sadie. 'I forgot to charge the battery. And I've been out all day.'

'Maybe you'd better come in,' said Lewis. 'Tomorrow morning, and we can talk.'

So, just as she did when Eddie was first banged up, Sadie again went to Lewis's office. But this time she declined coffee. And this time she knew a whole lot more about the trouble she was in. 'What the hell do you mean by putting my house up for sale without a word?' she said, trying to keep the anger and frustration out of her voice.

'Strictly speaking it's Mr Ross's property,' replied Lewis. 'And the mortgage is well in arrears.'

'I'm going to sort that out,' said Sadie.

'But he called me from the prison, and gave me instructions.'

'Instructions not to tell me?'

'No. I had no idea, Mrs Ross. This is most disturbing. We've always had a good relationship. If I'd known, I would have delayed speaking to the agents. I only tried to get in touch with you so that they could gain access to make a proper valuation.'

'I don't want them in the house!' Sadie cried angrily.

'This is difficult Mrs Ross. I've had my instructions. Mr Ross was adamant.'

'And so am I. No one gets in.' And with that she stormed out of the office.

Communication with Eddie then became impossible. No phone calls. No visitor's order, and the letters she sent remained unanswered.

A young man from the estate agent called to value the place. Sadie explained what was going on, and although he was sympathetic, he was unmoved by her protestations, and she was forced to seduce him in the master bedroom to get him to agree to delay the sale as long as possible. He was nervous and inexperienced, and Sadie felt like shooting him and burying his body in the basement.

Things were definitely going downhill when she couldn't even get a decent fuck.

So she called up her closest friends, Kate, Niki and Poppy to see if they could help.

They met in a Cantonese restaurant in Custom House. A huge, lavish place where she'd been once with Eddie in better times, and which had booths down one side to allow for privacy. Sadie had ordered a table for four, and she sat next to Kate, whilst Poppy and Niki who had arrived together sat opposite. They hadn't all met since the trial and the first half hour was spent catching up, although they were each careful to keep their secrets to themselves.

Finally, when they'd been served their duck with pancakes and plum sauce, and the second bottle of wine was open, Sadie began to tell the truth. 'I'm broke, girls,' she said. 'Skint. Boracic. That fucking bastard Eddie spent every penny, or at least that's what he says. And now he's put the fucking house up for sale without a word.'

'Behind your back?' asked a stunned Poppy.

'Yeah. You're not surprised are you? Those men don't give a shit. Look at what Joseph done.'

Poppy nodded.

'But Eddie wouldn't do that,' said Kate. 'He's your husband. And that's where you live.'

Sadie laughed. 'That's what I thought too. But he'd found out what I was up to with those blokes. Fuck knows how. Some little shit probably saw me at it, and grassed me up. I was a bit careless, if you know what I mean.'

'We did warn you,' said Kate.

'I know. I suppose none of you lot let anything slip...'

'No chance,' said Kate. 'Me, tell Robbo? You're

having a laugh.'

Niki and Poppy both shook their heads emphatically. 'You know we would never do that, babe,' said Poppy in a soft voice.

'I didn't think so,' said Sadie. 'I know I can trust you girls.'

Poppy and Niki exchanged nervous glances and Kate looked studiously at the tablecloth, each of them thinking of their own clandestine lives.

'Eddie told me to get a job, what a laugh,' said Sadie. 'What could I do? Stack shelves at Asda for a minimum wage. That ain't going to get me out of the trouble I'm in. We owe everyone. I'm on the fucking run night and day.'

'I've got some dough,' said Kate. 'Not much. Maybe five thousand, but you're welcome.'

'Me too,' said Poppy. 'A few grand.'

'Sorry Sadie,' said Niki, 'but you know how I'm fixed.'

'I know love,' said Sadie. 'And thanks girls, but I need a small fortune. That'd be like putting a sticking plaster on a broken leg. But one thing Eddie did do. A sort of parting gesture was to tell me a about a blag he's planned. A four-hander, plus a couple of muppets.'

'What kind of blag?' asked Kate.

Sadie lowered her voice. 'A truck full of old money up for burning. From a bank. Millions.

Eddie gets fifty pence on the pound, no danger. The chaps are doing it. I saw your Connie,' she said to Niki. 'Cunt told me to fuck off. Sorry.'

'You don't have to apologise to me Sadie,' said Niki. 'You know what I think of him.'

'When?' asked Kate. 'When's it supposed to be going down?'

'Christ knows,' replied Sadie. 'When the inside man gives the word. I thought one of you might know.'

The other girls looked at each other. 'They're always about making mischief,' said Poppy. 'But you know they don't let us mere women in on what's happening.'

'Fuckers,' said Sadie.

The dishes were taken away and the next course served, and then the next bottle of wine opened, and things at the table were beginning to get a little messy. As all the previous tensions eased it was almost like old times, with Sadie cracking filthy jokes and eyeing-up the gorgeous young waiters. 'So what's happening girls?' said Sadie. 'Come on, I know you lot too well. There's something up, don't say there isn't. Is it something I did? I know I've been a bit of a stranger since Eddie went away, but there's reasons. Come on, there's no secrets here. You girls are my best friends. What's the story?'

29

Niki and Poppy had kept their affair a secret so far. They booked into expensive hotels for an afternoon whenever they could, but they both knew that eventually the truth would come out, and when it did, they were in for big problems. Poppy's credit card bill was hitting its ceiling, and when Joseph sussed that out, questions were going to be asked. Serious questions, such as why Poppy was checking into luxury hotels two or three times a week. Joseph may not have wanted her, but he certainly wouldn't want to lose face with his mates by letting her shag another man, let alone a woman. They had talked long and hard about what to do, and the only answer seemed to be to vanish.

Collect together what cash they could and disappear into the sunset. Poppy suggested South Wales, and Niki, who hadn't travelled in the UK very far, agreed. She didn't know Wales from a hole in the ground, but Poppy was convinced they could get lost there. But it was a risky business, and both the women knew that Connie for one wasn't going to take his wife running off lightly. And, like Joe, it would probably drive him into a murderous fury. Niki being the wife of one of his mates would make it even worse.

When they set off to lunch, they had no intentions of telling Sadie and Kate what was going on, but a combination of too much wine and the stress they were living under finally made them come clean.

When Sadie asked what was going on, Poppy put her hand on Niki's and said nervously, 'We're together.'

Sadie and Kate looked across the table from Poppy to Niki and back again, like spectators at a tennis match. 'What?' said Sadie. 'What do you mean?'

'If this is a joke,' asked Kate. 'I don't get it.'

'Niki and I are lovers,' said Poppy. 'We love each other.'

'You're lesbians?' said Kate. 'But what about Joe? What about Connie?'

'Fuck them both,' said Niki. 'Joe only cares for his child and its mother. And Connie. He's a bastard who thinks because he paid for me to come here, he owns me. I hate him.'

'And I hate Joe,' said Poppy.

'But what are you going to do? Connie will kill you, Nik.'

'Not if I kill him first.'

'Are you having a laugh?' asked Kate, concerned for her friend's sanity. 'He's a maniac.'

'So am I,' said Niki. She picked up her handbag, fished inside and came out with a long bladed knife. One side had a saw edge, the other a cutter. The handle was bound with tape and it was stained a rusty brown.

'What are you doing with that?' said Sadie. 'You'll have us nicked. Are you crazy?'

'If you like,' said Niki. 'I may be crazy, but if Connie tries to stop me going, or comes after us, I'll cut his throat. And the same goes for Joe. I've done it before, and I'll do it again.' She dropped the knife amongst the dishes and cutlery on the table where it lay as dark and dangerous as a shark in a swimming pool.

'What the hell is that? And what do you mean, you've done it before?' exclaimed Kate.

'What I say,' said Niki. 'Don't underestimate me.'

'I don't get this,' said Sadie. 'When did this

happen? Going the other way I mean.'

'A few weeks ago,' said Poppy.

'And you're going to fuck off together?'

'That's the plan,' said Poppy.

'Where?'

'Far away from here.'

'And that money you offered me.'

'That's our pot,' said Poppy. 'It's not much, but it'll get us started.'

'And you'd have given it to me?'

'If it helped. You've been a mate,' said Poppy. 'We'd have found some other way to get some money.'

'I don't believe this,' said Sadie. 'What about you Kate?'

'I've got someone too,' Kate blurted as she poured more wine. 'And put that bloody thing away Niki. It's giving me the creeps. Is that blood?'

Niki nodded, and slid the knife back into her bag.

'Hold on,' said Sadie, grabbing Kate's arm. 'What do you mean you've got someone too?'

'I met someone. Well, he met me. He nicked me for hoisting up West weeks ago.'

'A copper?' Sadie exploded. 'You're going out with a fucking copper?'

'I wasn't going to tell,' said Kate. 'But when Poppy and Niki owned up... Well. I've told you now and that's all there is to it.'

'Fuck me,' said Sadie. 'This is like waking up and finding yourself in the land of Oz. Let's get another fucking bottle, and you can tell me everything. And Niki, did you really kill someone with that knife?'

Niki nodded. 'If you like I'll tell you about it.'

And she did.

30

Kate told the other three about being given a pull, and what had subsequently occurred. The only thing she left out was that Ali was Asian. In fact she never mentioned his name. 'And he took you out to lunch?' said Sadie. 'Cheek of the man. Then up to a hotel room.'

'Seemed like a good idea at the time,' said Kate. 'And at least he doesn't raise his hand to me like Robbo. He's kind and gentle.'

'He obviously raises something though,' said Sadie with a dirty laugh. 'You dirty bitch. Looks like you three are getting a bit of the other, and there's me all alone.'

'What about your blokes?' asked Poppy. 'You

were always at it.'

'Soon as the money ran out, so did they,' said Sadie. 'Fuckers. Or not, as the case may be.'

'Men,' the other three chorused in unison, and they all burst out laughing, relaxed and drunk from the copious amounts of wine.

'I don't believe all this,' said Sadie, as the waiter popped the cork out of the sixth, or was it the seventh bottle of Chardonnay? She waved away his offer of a taste. 'If it ain't right we'll let you know,' she said. 'Just leave it.'

When their glasses were filled they tapped the glassware and toasted each other drunkenly. 'Christ,' said Sadie to Kate. 'What would happen if Robbo found out you were screwing a bill?'

'He'd kill me too,' she said.

'Looks like us girls are living close to the edge,' said Sadie. 'And all our blokes have pissed on us one way or another.'

'Well, we're pissing on them now,' said Kate.

'Listen,' said Sadie, lowering her voice again. 'I've had an idea. This robbery. Why don't we piss on them once and for all?'

'What do you mean?' asked Poppy.

'I know the details. Or at least most of them.' She briefly explained what was going to happen according to Eddie's plan. 'Now, you three are going to know when something's kicking off. You must. You know what they're like when they've got something big planned. You could find out exactly when the drop off is going to be. When they've got the clean money. We could take it off them.'

'Oh yeah,' said Kate. 'What with? Niki's knife, and a couple of chopsticks off the table?'

'I've got weapons,' said Sadie. 'And enough ammunition to start world war three.'

'What weapons?' asked Niki, suddenly interested.

'Three Glock handguns and an Uzi semi-automatic.'

'Where did you get them?' asked Kate.

'Eddie's got them in safe deposit boxes.'

'Have you ever used a gun?' asked Niki.

'Not until the other day. I loaded one of the pistols and went down Epping Forest for a practice. I'm still half deaf.'

'Guns scare me,' said Kate.

'Me too,' Poppy chimed in. 'It's a mad idea.'

'So is running off to sheep shagging, wild and woolly Wales,' said Sadie.

'It's not so mad,' said Niki. 'I could teach you. I know weapons. I've fired an Uzi. Poppy, what about it?'

'If you say so Niki. I don't like it, but whatever you want to do I'll back you up. You know that.'

'Are you scared?'

'Terrified.'

'Don't worry, I'll protect you. I love you, I'm not going to let anything hurt you.'

'You're all crazy,' said Kate.

'Coming from a gangster's wife who sleeping with a copper, that's rich,' said Sadie.

'Suppose you're right,' said Kate, finishing her glass of wine and shaking the empty bottle. 'Do you reckon they do Irish coffee here?'

31

When the girls finally staggered out into the late afternoon sunshine they agreed to make a meet in two days time at Sadie's place. 'If I've still got a fucking place,' she said as she headed for her car. 'Unless the bleedin' bailiffs come in, or some cunt puts in an offer.'

'Show 'em your stocking tops,' said Poppy. 'That'll give 'em something to think about.'

'Give 'em a shag,' said Sadie. 'Done that already.'

'How do you mean?'

Sadie explained and the other girls almost collapsed with laughter.

'Glad you think it's funny,' said Sadie. 'Worst fuck of my life.'

Niki grabbed her by the arm as she was getting into the motor. 'Are you going to get those guns?' she said.

'Yeah,' replied Sadie.

'Want us to come with you?'

'No. Going in mob-handed we'll be remembered. I'll slob myself up a bit. Don't worry, it'll be all right.'

'Just be careful. I hear the British cops don't like automatic weapons.'

'I'll be good,' said Sadie. 'See you Thursday.'

The next day she dressed in an old Juicy velour tracksuit, greased her hair down and wore big sunglasses when she went to the two banks where the guns and ammo were stored. She took an old rucksack and a leather holdall with her.

At the first bank she carefully put the weapons into the back pack and transferred them to her car. She felt that all eyes were upon her as she went from the bank to the car park, but all was well.

At the second bank the official who brought in her drawer said. 'This is heavy, feels like a lead weight.'

How right you are thought Sadie, but she said, 'Family jewels love. Things have gone pear shaped. Got to hock the lot. Don't worry, it won't weigh much when you take it back.' And it didn't, as she'd transferred all the ammunition to the holdall which she could hardly lift, it weighed so much. But she managed, and drove home feeling confident the plan would go off without a hitch—as long as the other girls did their bit and didn't chicken out.

The next morning Kate, Poppy and Niki arrived at the house as arranged.

Sadie had hidden the guns in the basement utility room, and they all convened downstairs. Niki went straight to the ammunition and started to load the guns. The other three could hardly believe how swiftly and expertly she loaded the clips. The bullets seemed to just spring into the magazines. 'You've done that before,' said Sadie.

'A thousand times,' replied Niki, as she slammed the Uzi's thirty round clip home, tugged back the bolt, and set the gun to full auto. She hefted it upright, and the other three suddenly realised what a dangerous woman she was as she spun round to aim the gun at Sadie's washer/drier.

'Careful,' said Sadie. 'That ain't paid for yet.'

'It will be,' said Niki, and she carefully put the Uzi on top of the machine. 'Right,' she said. 'Now it's you lot's turn.'

'Bloody hell,' said Kate as she gingerly accepted a Glock and an empty magazine. 'What do I do now?'

'Push the bullets into the mag just like I did,' said

Niki, and Kate clumsily attempted the feat.

'No,' said Niki. 'That won't do. Sadie, you got scissors and an emery board?'

'Course,' replied Sadie and dived into her handbag.

'No,' said Kate, realising what was going to happen. 'No.'

'You'll never manage with those nails,' said Niki. 'Give me your hand.'

'This manicure set me back a ton,' wailed Kate, as Niki grabbed her left hand and chopped off the expensive acrylic fingernails she wore. Then she did the same with the right and tossed Kate the emery.

'File 'em down short.'

'Robbo'll kill me.'

'I doubt it,' said Niki. 'But maybe you can kill *him* if you learn to shoot straight.'

32

'The next thing is to shoot these little babies,' said Niki, picking up the Uzi again and stroking it like a pet cat. 'Where should we do it?'

'Well, not my back garden,' said Sadie. 'Might upset the neighbours. How about that place in Epping Forest I found? It was quiet. Never saw a soul.'

'You took a big risk,' said Niki. 'I suppose you used your own car.'

Sadie nodded.

'Right,' said Niki. 'The forest is good. But look at us. We need to keep a low profile. And you Kate. Not in those shoes. You got anything a bit more suitable for a walk through the woods?' she said to Sadie.

'What's wrong with my shoes?' said Kate. 'These are Jimmy Choos.'

'Exactly,' said Niki.

'I've got some Timberlands upstairs,' said Sadie. 'You're a six aren't you Kate?'

Kate nodded.

'Great.'

'And we'll steal a car,' said Niki.

'What?' said Sadie.

'It won't be as nice as yours. Something older, that I can get into fast.'

'You steal cars?' said Kate.

'Sure. Who doesn't? And we'll all need gloves. You got some Sade?'

'I can do that. Just as well I'm a fashion victim. Or was.'

Poppy just looked on silently. There was a lot her friends didn't know about Niki, but they were beginning to learn.

In her borrowed boots, leather gloves, and a Barbour waxed jacket, Kate fitted in with the others who had dressed for a day in the country. They took the guns out to Sadie's SUV, once more packed away in the rucksack, with all spare magazines loaded.

'Is there a supermarket close?' asked Niki. 'With a car park?'

'Yeah,' replied Sadie. 'But I do my weekly shop

there, and it's loaded with CCTV.'

'Let me worry about that,' said Niki.

Sadie drove to the supermarket and Niki hopped out of her car at the entrance. 'Drive on,' she said. 'Then park up where you can. I'll flash the lights when I see you, and we'll find somewhere to dump your car.'

'You're confident,' said Kate.

'Trust me,' Niki said, and then she was gone.

Sadie did as she was told, and drove into a lay by a couple of miles up the road. Within minutes, a nondescript Japanese hatchback flashed its lights and pulled in behind. Niki was at the wheel. She got out and ran up to Sadie's window. 'Easy,' she said. 'Might as well leave yours here. We'll pick it up later. Get the guns and be quick.'

The girls left the SUV, Poppy carrying the rucksack full of weapons, and piled into the hatchback which smelt of cigarettes and BO. 'Nice,' said Kate.

Niki got behind the wheel and pulled back onto the main road.

Sadie gave her directions to Epping and as they sped along the main road, Poppy said. 'What's the sentence do you think, driving a stolen car full of guns?'

'Christ,' said Kate.

'Just asking,' said Poppy with a grin. 'This is fun.'

It was several miles later that things started going pear shaped. A white Transit van decided to pass Niki and cut her up severely as he flashed her a V-sign. Niki said something in Russian that sounded obscene and took off after the van. 'Leave it,' said Sadie.

'Will I fuck. Bastard man,' said Niki and smashed her foot down on the accelerator and rocketed past the truck, pulled in hard and fast, nearly sending it off the road. She reached round and pulled the Uzi from the rucksack.

'No,' screamed Kate as the driver got out of the van, a huge, bald-headed man in T-shirt and jeans. Niki jumped out of the hatchback, stood in the middle of the road and pulled the trigger of the machine pistol which punched thirty rounds straight through the engine block and windscreen. The driver stood open mouthed and looked at the wreck of his transport, as water, oil and petrol ran into the road in a steaming torrent. Niki ran up to him and jabbed the hot barrel of her gun into his ear. 'Reckon I've got one more bullet for you,' she hissed, as he almost fainted and a big brown patch appeared at the back of his trousers. She slammed him hard in the head with the gun, then ran back to the hatchback, leapt in, chucked the Uzi to Poppy in the back seat and roared off. 'Well, that one works for sure. God, but that felt good,' she said.

'Jesus Niki,' said Sadie. 'That could've screwed us well and truly. What would've happened if another car had come past?'

'I'd have shot the engine out. Simple.'

'You can't shoot the whole world.'

'I don't know,' replied Niki with a manic grin. 'Long as there's enough ammunition.'

'Are we going to have trouble with you?' asked Sadie, not amused.

'I'll try to do better in future,' said Niki. 'But no promises.'

'Do you think he got our number?' asked Kate.

'I doubt it,' replied Niki. 'He was too busy shitting his pants. But maybe we'd better get another car just in case.'

'What about your prints?' asked Sadie. 'They're all over the cartridge cases you left lying in the road, aren't they?'

'Never had my prints taken' replied Niki. 'What sort of a girl do you think I am? Now let's get some new transport?'

33

And that's exactly what she did. Not far down the road was a branch railway station with a pay and display car park rammed with commuter's cars. She pulled up outside, shooed the other girls out of the hatchback, drove in, parked, and joined them almost immediately in an ten-year-old Ford Granada. 'It's not much,' she said. 'But it's got a full tank.'

'All aboard the Skylark,' said Poppy as they got inside, just as a police car with blues flashing and twos screaming roared past in the direction they'd come from, but didn't as much as slow down.

'That was quick,' said Kate. 'Just as well we got rid of that other motor.'

'Should've nicked his phone,' said Niki. 'Right then. Where to from here? And what the bloody hell is the Skylark?'

Nobody bothered to explain.

They got to the forest and Sadie showed them the burnt tree where she'd practised her shooting. The Granada wouldn't make the rough track that she'd used in her four wheel drive, so they abandoned it. With Niki carrying the rucksack they went into the woods which once again were deserted, without so much as a man walking his dog. 'Told you,' said Sadie. 'Not a soul about.'

'Lucky for them,' said Niki. 'Otherwise I might have been forced to kill them.'

'You're a happy little soul, Niki, you know that?' said Kate.

Niki deigned not to reply.

They fired off the rounds they'd brought with them, and even Kate took an interest as her bullets chopped lumps out of the dead tree. 'See,' said Niki. 'I knew you could do it.'

'I still don't know if we can carry this off,' said Kate as they drove back to where Sadie had left her car in the lay by, this time collecting the spent cartridge cases, passing the scene of Niki's shootout, where the white van had been shoved off the road and was covered in police tape, the road next to it stained with oil, petrol and antifreeze.

'Served the fucker right,' said Niki. 'He won't be picking on women drivers for a bit,' and they all laughed hysterically, but through fear rather than hilarity.

'It's the timing that worries me,' said Sadie, suddenly serious. 'For all we know they might be doing the job today.'

'Not Joe,' said Poppy. 'He's off playing golf. Should've seen the state of him this morning in his plus fours. Fucking twat. He looked just like Ainsley, that dopey cook off the telly.'

'And Robbo always gets amorous when something's going off,' said Kate. 'Which he isn't, thank God.'

'Not getting any nookie, love?' said Sadie. 'Join the club.'

'Only the boyfriend,' Poppy piped up. 'Still having it off with Her Majesty's constabulary Kate?'

Kate blushed scarlet. 'All right,' she said. 'Leave it out.'

'But we've got to know,' said Sadie. 'I mean it. All this is a waste of time if they do the job without us knowing.'

'We could just take the money after,' said Kate. 'One by one.'

'No,' said Niki. 'We do them all at the same time and get lost. We need the cash all in one place.

Right?'

'Right,' said Sadie. 'So you lot need to keep your eyes and ears open. Right?'

The other three nodded agreement as Niki pulled up next to Sadie's SUV. They loaded it up, left the Granada and went back to Sadie's place.

'Now remember girls,' she said before they left. 'Eyes and ears open. We need to know every detail.'

And with that, they parted.

34

Kate, Poppy and Niki got their spy hats on. It was a risky business. Niki went through her small house from top to bottom. She checked out the room that Connie called his office, although he was rarely in it. All she turned up was a bunch of paid bills, and not much else. Connie kept things close to his chest, and she wasn't surprised. As far as making small talk, that rarely happened any more, and she knew he'd smell a rat if she started on with the third degree, so she ended up admitting defeat. What she would have liked to do was borrow the Uzi, stick it in his ear like she'd done to the white van man, and get the truth out of him that way. She could hardly wait for a chance to get even with him. And she knew that only one of them would walk away alive.

Poppy came up against the same brick wall. Joseph was another closed-mouthed man, and when she met Niki for an afternoon of sex, she told her she was none the wiser.

In fact it was Kate who got the first inkling of the job, and it happened in the worst way.

One morning, a week or so later, as they were having breakfast and watching *BBC 24* Robbo said, 'I've got a meet this morning. Christ knows how long I'll be.'

'Something important?' asked Kate.

'None of your fucking business. Keep your nose out.'

'Sorry.'

'You will be. Now, have I got a clean shirt?'

'On a hanger in your wardrobe.'

'Good girl.'

'Where are you going to be?' Kate tried to sound as innocent as possible.

'Brick Lane. Some poncy bar or other. Used to be good down there before all those wankers started hanging out. Dinner for a nicker. Now look at the fucking place.'

'Who you meeting?'

'Some geezer. In the building trade. Fucking Paki.'

And that was when Kate got the first sniff. 'What do you want a builder for?'

'I told you. None of your business.' And he finished his toast, left the dishes for Kate to clear away and went upstairs to get dressed.

After he'd left, she put on an old Burberry mac, pushed her shock of red hair up under a baseball cap, left off her make up, and put on a pair of large lensed sunglasses. She caught her reflection as she left the house and laughed at herself, all dressed up like a spy from a bad movie, and caught the tube to Aldgate. A poncy bar, he'd said, and there were plenty of those to choose from. She wandered the Lane avoiding young Asians trying to get her to take an early lunch with offers of cheap food and booze, until she saw Robbo sitting in the window of a bar with a bottle of beer in his hand. He was alone. But not for long. She looked in the window of a sari shop opposite, using it as a mirror, when who should walk along the road, turn into the bar and greet her husband, but Ali S. Karim, dressed in a leather jacket and jeans with a couple of day's growth of beard on his face.

Kate almost fainted as the pair shook hands and Ali fetched more beers from the bar.

Kate fled, head down, her mind in turmoil. What the fuck's going on? she thought. What are those two doing together? And why?

There was only one thing for it. She called Ali on his mobile and got his voice mail. 'You fucker,' she said. 'Phone me, as soon as you get this.'

'This is rare,' said Ali, when he phoned her later that day. 'You letting me call you. Fancy a fuck?'

'What are you doing meeting my husband?' Kate demanded.

There was a long silence. 'How do you know?' he eventually asked. 'Did he tell you?'

'What? That he's meeting my bit on the side... Do you think I'd be able to talk? I'd be in the fucking London having surgery on my broken jaw. Now what's going on?'

'Not on the phone?'

'Where then?'

'Up west. Out of the area. Tonight?'

'No not tonight stupid. Tomorrow. That little pub where we met before in Beaufort Street. Remember?'

'How could I forget? That was a beautiful afternoon.'

'Don't piss me about Ali. Don't be a cunt all your life. Take a day off. Tomorrow. Opening time, and don't be fucking late.' And she killed the phone.

* * *

What had occurred was that, after Eddie's trial, Ali went to his bosses and strongly suggested that the remainder of the gang should be treated as serious targets. He knew, and they knew that Robbo,

Connie and Joseph had been the others in the mail van robbery, and it angered him to see them sticking two fingers up at the law because of lack of proof. His bosses agreed, and gave Ali *carte blanche* to bring them in. It was just what he wanted, so he plugged himself into the villain grapevine that still operated in London. It was a loose network fuelled by public phone boxes, and meetings in tatty boozers and deserted car parks. Its language was a mixture of modern street and old rhyming slang. No mobiles. The air had ears. Ali slid down into the underworld and kept his eyes and ears open. His cover was that of an Asian fixer who'd fallen out with his cohorts up north and had to relocate to London in a hurry with more or less what he had on his back. He was skint and needed an earner fast. He almost lived in his car for weeks, hanging out with anyone who looked bent enough to be in the know about what was happening, and getting as many knock backs as usable information. A lot of the gangsters were old-school east end, and didn't want to deal with some bolshy Paki bloke. But he persevered, and took the shit without fighting back, until one afternoon in a dodgy pub in Rotherhithe he heard about a face who needed some heavy earth moving equipment for a bit of lucrative work. Ali butted in that he could get anything in that line from a mate in Birmingham, delivered fast, no questions asked, as long as the fee was right. Ali told the publican that he had worked building sites and on the M62 road widening scheme, and was a top driver.

He heard nothing for a few days, until on a further trip to the pub the boss told him that someone wanted a meet. 'You'd better've been straight with me mate,' the publican warned. 'This bloke takes no prisoners.'

'Who is he?' asked Ali.

The publican looked up and down the almost deserted room and whispered. 'His name's Robbo. That's all you need to know. I'm going to bell him now, and he'll ring back on my private line. Keep it short, and no fucking names.'

The publican vanished into the back. A few minutes later Ali heard a phone ring, and the bloke stuck his head through the door and motioned for Ali to join him. He had his hand over the receiver. 'Here you go,' he said. 'And make it quick.'

Ali took the phone and said, 'Yeah?'

'You the Paki?' said a gruff voice.

'That's right.'

'Brick Lane tomorrow morning, eleven. Soul Bar. Know it?'

'I'll find it.'

'Be there.'

'How will I know you?'

'I'll wear a fucking carnation and carry the *Financial Times*,' said the voice. 'It'll be quiet. Use your fucking initiative.' And the line went dead.

Ali went back through to the bar. 'OK?' asked the publican.

'No problem.'

'Make mine a double. And remember me if there's any bunce about.'

'Oh, I'll remember you,' said Ali, dropping a twenty on the bar. 'Don't worry about that.' And he left the pub, wondering how to talk his bosses into sanctioning obtaining a hundred-grand's worth of heavy plant machinery.

* * *

The meeting went off as arranged. Robbo arrived early, and sat with a bottle of beer at a table by the window. As he'd prophesied, at that time of day the place was almost empty, with just a couple at a table by the kitchen, and the occasional worker popping in for a take out beverage.

Ali was nervous as he walked down Brick Lane, and didn't recognise the figure standing opposite staring into the window of a sari shop. But she recognised him.

He went into the restaurant and of course he recognised Robbo straight away, but managed to look a little lost as he looked round. Robbo stared straight at him and Ali went across to the table.

'Robbo?' he asked almost hesitantly.

'You the Paki?'

Ali swallowed his resentment at the remark and instead nodded. 'That's me.'

'Name?' demanded Robbo.

'Ali,' said Ali. He'd figured he might as well tell the truth as he'd probably be called Ali anyway, even if his name was Prince Charles. Fucking cockneys, thought they were so funny.

'OK Ali,' said Robbo. 'Get the beers in.'

Ali did as he was told and returned with two bottles of Cobra. 'Thought you lot didn't drink,' said Robbo.

'Some of us do.' Ali remembered back to his first meeting with Kate, when she'd asked the same thing. It gave him a thrill to look into Robbo's face and know that he'd fucked his wife.

'Well thank Christ for that.'

Although he'd studied photos and seen Robbo from a distance at the Bailey, close up Ali saw how dangerous the man was. How did Kate put up with it? he thought. Robbo's face was as expressive as a skull, the skin drawn tight across the bones, his body had a hardness that was obvious even fully dressed, and his knuckles were white with old scars.

'You know what I want?' said Robbo after a moment.

'Heavy plant.'

'And you can get it?'

'For a price. Bulldozers are extra.'

'No fucking jokes,' said Robbo with menace in his voice. 'This is fucking serious. I need two JCB mechanical shovels.'

'Easy,' said Ali and prayed that it would be. 'When?'

'Soon.'

'How soon?'

'Too many fucking questions.'

'Sorry.'

'And you can drive them. Teach someone else?' asked Robbo.

'No problem.'

'How much then?'

'Are they coming back?'

'I said no jokes.'

'I'm serious too.'

'No chance. They'll be burned.'

'Then I'd say ten grand the pair. Up front.'

'I won't argue.'

'What's the job?'

'Need to know son, and you don't. Not yet. I don't know you. My mates don't know you. Nobody knows you. You just turn up out of the blue. I'd say that looks a bit suss. You need checking out before we get all friendly. And you look like you've been living in a tree.'

'Temporary difficulties.'

'Then get a fucking wash, and stick around that boozer. I'll be in touch.' And with that he left his beer and walked out.

Ali sat back with a satisfied look on his face. Result. At least, so far.

35

The pub was empty when Kate arrived the next day, and had that smell that pubs do at that time of day. A mixture of stale beer, stale cigarettes and disinfectant. A barman stood looking bored behind the counter, but cheered up when she walked in and ordered a fruit juice. Ali got there a few minutes later, and the barman pulled a face when he greeted Kate with a kiss. She didn't respond, just took her drink to a table by the door as Ali asked for a pint of lager.

'Cheers,' he said when he had sat down opposite her and lit a cigarette.

'Don't fucking give me cheers,' she replied. 'What was all that about?'

'What?'

'You know what. Don't fuck about. You and Robbo, having a cosy chat. Thick as thieves.'

Ali smiled at that and sipped his drink.

'Why?' she demanded. 'I'm losing my patience here.'

'I can't tell you Kate.'

'Was it about me?'

Ali laughed. 'No,' he replied. 'Not about you. Not everything's about you love.'

'What then?'

'I told you Kate, I can't say.'

'Does he know who you are?'

'What, a copper or your boyfriend?'

'Either. Both. Just tell me.'

He shrugged.

'So I assume neither. If he knew you were a copper, he'd rather kill you than drink with you socially. If he knew you were my boyfriend, he'd kill me, or both of us. So it must be business.'

'That makes sense.'

'Are you on the bung with him?'

Ali smiled. 'No. Not on the bung.'

'So what?'

'It's complicated.'

'I could make it more complicated. I could tell him who you are?'

'And that you know me, and that you were

spying on him. I take it you weren't down there buying bagels for lunch.'

Kate was silent.

'So why were you spying on him? Did you think he'd got a bird on the side? I didn't think you cared.'

'I don't.'

'So why?' he pressed.

'Now it's your turn to mind your own business.'

'No, Kate. This is important. I mean it.'

'Wait a minute. You told him you were in the building trade.'

'How do you know that?'

'Because he let it slip.'

'And that's why you followed him?'

'Maybe.'

'Tell me Kate.'

'Are you undercover?'

Ali just pulled a face.

'Christ, you're going to do that job with him.'

'What job?'

'Don't play innocent Ali. The job that needs two JCBs. That job.'

'What do you know about it?'

'Just about everything.'

'You shouldn't.'

'Maybe. But I do. When is it?'

'So you don't know everything.'

'Tell me.'

'No.'

'I'll grass you up Ali.'

'And take the consequences?' he said.

'Whatever.'

'I don't believe you.'

'Then I'll get somebody else to do it.'

'And I could grass you, us, up.'

'And take the consequences?' Kate said back to him, echoing Ali's words.

'*Touché.*'

'So tell me.'

'I don't think so.'

'Soon, obviously.'

Ali's expression said nothing.

'It must be soon.'

'Why do you want to know anyway?'

'So it's true.'

'Tell me Kate.' Ali said again, gently.

'Because we're going to rip them off.'

'Do what?'

'Rob the robbers.'

'Who?'

'Us girls.'

'Which girls?'

'Eddie's wife, Joe's wife, Connie's wife and me.'

Ali laughed. 'You're going to take four of the most dangerous men in London's money? You must be having a laugh.'

'Three men. Eddie's in prison remember. You were there. You know as well as I do. For all you know they might've seen you.'

'I made sure they didn't. Only you. Anyway, we all look the same, us Asians. They haven't got a clue. I was booted and suited that day. Now I'm a greasy Paki in a leather jacket, who can get hold of some buckshee heavy machinery. Bent as a nine-bob note, me. Your old man put out the word. And I heard about it. Went to my guv'nors and they agreed that I should do the business. Simple.'

'And you're going to get them nicked.'

'That's the plan. But now *you* know...'

'Then help us. We could go away together. There'd be enough money to last us the rest of our lives. You want to be with me. You've told me enough times.'

'An interesting idea Kate. But how do I know I can trust you?'

'You don't.'

He smiled. 'OK,' he said. 'Just say I agree. How do you intend to carry out this audacious plan?'

'You first. Will you do it?'

Ali sat back and sipped at his drink. He was becoming less and less in love with the job every day. The racism, the e-mails calling him a dirty little wog stealing white men's jobs. 'I'll think about it,' he said. 'Don't worry, there's plenty of time. It won't be for weeks. Trust me.'

'I suppose I have to,' said Kate.

'Now, I'm off today. Fancy going somewhere quiet?'

'If you do.'

'Always.'

36

After she left Ali, Kate called Sadie. She wasn't looking forward to telling her what was going on, but it was the only way. 'What's up love?' asked Sadie. 'You got something for me?'

'Yeah.'

'You sound rotten. You coming down with something?'

'No.'

'So tell me.'

'Not on the phone. We have to meet.'

'Sounds important.' There was a note of excitement in Sadie's voice.

'It is.'

'When?'

'Soon as.'

'Today?'

'No. Robbo'll get the hump. Tomorrow morning?'

'Sure. Where?'

'Bluewater.'

'Sounds OK. What time?'

'About eleven.'

'OK by me. Look I'll ring you when I'm there, and we'll find somewhere quiet.'

Somewhere quiet was a coffee shop on the first floor mezzanine. Kate was already there when Sadie phoned. 'I'm just parking up,' she said.

Kate gave her directions and ordered more coffee, and within a few minutes Sadie joined her. 'Go on then,' said Sadie when she was settled. 'What's the problem?'

'You're not going to believe this.'

'Try me.'

Kate was close to tears as she told Sadie about seeing Ali with Robbo, and their subsequent meeting. 'He's what?' said Sadie.

'He's going in as a builder. He can get those dump trucks.'

'And he's a Paki.'

'Don't Sade.'

'Christ on a bicycle. I don't believe this.'

'Believe it.'

'And you told him about the plan?'

'It was the only way.'

'And he's going to help us get the cash?'

'So he said. When I had his cock in my mouth.'

'Fuckers will say anything for a blow job.'

'I know.'

'Did you believe him?'

Kate shrugged.'

'And you had a shag?'

'Two. But he's not the same as he was. He's gone all nasty. Like he's in control now.'

'That's men for you. Fuck me Kate, you are a one.'

'So what do we do?'

'It's obvious. We use him, like he's used you. And then we stitch him up too.'

'You reckon?'

'I know my love. Now you're going to have to box clever. Get everything out of him that you can. OK?'

'I will.'

'And for Christ's sake be careful.'

'I'll do that too.'

* * *

Meanwhile Ali was busy trying to convince his boss that he had to obtain two JCB earth moving machines. And it wasn't easy.

'What the hell do they need them for?'

demanded DCI John Loomis, from behind his desk at Scotland Yard. He was an old school type of copper, more Regan than Morse. More seventies pop than grand opera.

'Well, I don't think they're going to be digging a swimming pool,' replied Ali. 'It's a blag.'

'Of course it's a bloody blag. But what? The top layer of the M4?'

'If it was just one I'd say ATMs. But these blokes are serious villains. It's a tin can of some kind. They like doing cash in transit. Don't forget the mail van.'

'As if I could. Bastards. But two. Christ, do you know how much these things cost?'

'I've Googled them.'

'You bloody well would. Are we going to get them back?'

Ali crossed his fingers behind his back. 'Sure Guv. I guarantee it.' In a pig's ear'ole, he thought. But tough. The Met could afford it. They had money to burn. Always paying out for some mistake or another. Fuck 'em. 'And I'll need a low loader,' he added.

'Why?'

'Well I can drive one. I know how. But not two.'

'How the hell do you know how to drive one?'

'Gap year. I worked building sites.'

Loomis gave him the sort of look that said he

didn't approve of things like gap years, but he relented. 'Oh shit,' he said. 'We'll have to hire the fucking things I suppose. What about my budget?'

Sod your budget, thought Ali. I hope I won't be around to sign the chit.

'Go ahead then,' said Loomis. 'But take it easy for Christ's sake.'

37

And, then, when it seemed things couldn't get any more complicated for her, Kate got a phone call from her eldest brother, Ben. 'Dad's ill,' he said.

'Something serious I hope.'

'Don't make jokes.'

'That's no joke,' she said. 'I mean it.'

'He's dying.'

'Break out the party hats.'

'Don't be like that, Katie.'

'What should I be like?'

'He's asking for you,' said Ben.

'Tough titty.'

'He's changed, sis.'

'Into a frog?'

'Whatever you feel about him Kate, he's still your dad.'

'He gave up that job years ago.'

'You haven't seen him darlin'.'

'And I don't want to.'

'How long's it been?'

'Not long enough.' Four years to be precise, she thought. And she wished it had been longer.

'Katie, please. He's at the house. He discharged himself from hospital and went home.'

'With that bimbo?'

'No. She fucked off when he was first diagnosed.'

'What is it?'

'Cirrhosis of the liver.'

'Painful?'

'Very.'

'Good fucking job,' said Kate, harshly.

'You don't mean that.'

'Yes I do. Remember the way he was with mum, and me. I suppose you don't. You boys were all right. He worshipped you.'

'And you. And mum.'

'He had a funny way of showing it. The thick end of his fist, as I remember.'

'We did what we could. He laid into us too.'

'And what did you do? Fucked off as soon as you turned 18. Left us with him.'

'Yeah, I know. And I'm sorry, sis. But he has changed. He's got religion.'

'Now you are taking the piss. Johnny Wade on his knees in front of God. That I would like to see.'

'Come and see him then. He hasn't got long.'

She hesitated.

'He's your blood,' Ben pressed. 'Come on love, do the right thing.'

'OK, Ben. I give in. When?'

'Soon as. He's going fast. You won't recognise him.'

'Tomorrow?'

'Good girl.'

She hung up and poured herself a stiff drink. She was all alone again as usual, and she sat down and thought about the past, and the present, and wondered what the future would bring. Nothing good, she thought. The way things were going.

She told Robbo what Ben had said, and he asked her if she wanted company.

'No. I'm better off on my own.'

'Well, give him my best,' he said. 'I always got on with the old man.'

'You didn't have to live with him.'

'That's true. Anyway, I've got things to do myself.'

I just bet you have, she thought.

The next morning she got up early, leaving Robbo

in bed, showered and dressed in jeans and a leather jacket, had a sparse breakfast which she couldn't eat, her stomach tied up in knots at the thought of seeing her father after such a long time. Around ten she got into her car and drove to the old house in Plaistow where she'd known such sorrow, and where she'd watched her mother dying.

Nothing much had changed there. It was a big place for the area, a corner property hidden by high walls and hedges. As she parked outside and walked up the front path she noticed that the flower beds that had been Dolly's pride and joy, blooming with bright fragrant flowers, were now unkempt and choked with weeds.

She knocked on the front door and Ben opened it. 'Hello darlin',' he said. 'Long time.' He went to embrace her, but she backed off. 'Like I said, not long enough,' she said. She hadn't seen Ben for years either.

'Be like that then.'

'What did you expect? Hearts and flowers?'

'You've grown hard Katie.'

'I had good teachers.'

'Listen,' he said as they stood in the hall. 'We did what we could. The boys and me. But we had our own lives. You were just a kid.'

'Old enough to know what was going on with mum.'

'I'm sorry about that. But you know what she was like. She wouldn't hear a word against him.'

'She was stupid.'

'Don't talk about mum like that.'

She ignored his comment. 'Where is he?' she asked.

'In bed. You want some tea?'

'If you like. Anybody else here?'

'No. We take it in turns. We've all got work and kids. You've never seen my youngest. I've got a photo.'

He pulled out his wallet and showed Kate a photo of a pretty little girl in a party frock. 'Her second birthday,' he said. 'You could've come.'

'Yeah,' she said. 'But I didn't. Now, how about that tea?'

38

Ben made a pot in the kitchen. Kate remembered being a young girl, sitting on the wooden chair in the corner whilst Dolly cooked and poured out her troubles to her. The kitchen hadn't changed much either. Just a bit more used. Like us all, thought Kate.

She sat at the table as Ben poured her a cup then heard a knocking on the ceiling above. 'He's awake,' said Ben. 'I'll take him up a cuppa, and tell him you're here.'

He poured a third cup and went upstairs. He was gone for ten minutes, and Kate drank the bitter brew. It reminded her of the bitter times when she'd lived at home, and the fact that Ben had never been able to make a decent cuppa to save his life. She smoked a cigarette to calm her shaking hands and stubbed it out in her saucer.

When Ben returned, he said. 'He's going to have a wash and shave, and take his meds. He's glad you're here.'

'I'm not.'

'Leave it out sis. Just for now. You don't know what he's like these days.'

'Oh yes I do.'

Ben shook his head, but said nothing.

Just like old times, Kate washed up her cup, dropping the cigarette butt into the rubbish bin. Old habits die hard, she thought. If you left crocks lying around when she lived here she got the sharp edge of Johnny's tongue, and sometimes worse.

Eventually there was more hammering on the ceiling, and Ben said. 'He's ready. He wants to see you on his own.'

Lucky me, thought Kate, but she didn't bother to say it.

She went out of the kitchen and climbed the familiar stairs to the first floor. Johnny and Dolly had shared the master bedroom, and she pushed open the door and looked inside. It was gloomy there, the curtains drawn, and smelled like a hospital. Sharp, with an overlying stink of bodily corruption, and Kate almost gagged. 'Is that you

Katie?' asked a familiar but weakened voice from the bed.

'It's me.'

'Come in girl.'

'Haven't you got a light in here?'

'It's not pretty.'

'Just put the light on Dad, I'll break my neck otherwise.'

She heard a fumble, then a dim bulb in the bedside lamp came on. Johnny Wade was propped up in bed by two pillows. His face was the colour of urine, and his eyes were like a pair of fried eggs in a face so gaunt she hardly recognised him. His once black hair was grey and thin and his hands on the covers shook uncontrollably. He saw the shock on her face and said. 'Told you.'

She looked around the familiar room now transformed into a hospital ward with an oxygen tank, a stand for a drip, a Zimmer frame, a TV mounted on brackets, and a table covered in pill boxes. 'Christ, Dad,' she said. 'It's like *Casualty* in here.'

'Ain't it just. Come close, let me see you.'

Kate did as she was bid and he peered at her closely. 'Christ. Just like your mother. Where you been girl? I've missed you.'

Kate almost laughed. 'Yeah, that's right Dad. You've had nobody to knock about.'

'That's not me any more. Come closer. Sit down.'

Kate went to his bedside and perched on the edge of the mattress. Johnny reached out a trembling hand. After a moment she took it. All the strength seemed to have gone out of him and it was like holding an old glove full of fish bones. Suddenly Kate was no longer frightened. She was the strong one now, and she could have broken his wrist like a breadstick.

'How long have you got Dad?' she asked.

'Not long love. Not long at all.'

'So what am I supposed to do?' Kate spat out.

'A bit of sympathy wouldn't hurt.'

'Like what you gave me and Mum. And the boys, for that matter.'

'I did my best. I fed and clothed the lot of you.'

'Out of what?'

'The same as your old man now. Don't get all righteous with me.'

'I hear that's what you've got,' she said. 'Religion, isn't it?'

For the first time she noticed a beaded rosary around his left wrist. 'Come on Dad, what's all that?'

'I was confirmed a Catholic.'

'Were you?'

'Did my stint as an altar boy until the priest started to fiddle with me. I gave him a smack and never went back to church.'

'Until now.'

'I need it. Listen Katie. Forget what's been between us. I need to talk.'

'To confess?'

'I done that already. The priest comes every few days.'

'But doesn't fiddle about I assume.'

'I'm a bit old and ugly for that these days.' He laughed. A dreadful sound that turned into a fit of coughing, and he put the oxygen mask over his face. 'Yeah. But I do need to confess to you. I know I treated you and Dolly bad. But we never expected you to come along, and when you did...'

'I wasn't wanted,' Kate finished for him.

'You were a jewel. We all loved you. But you went off the straight and narrow.'

'What the bloody hell do you know about the straight and narrow for Christ's sakes? All I did was because of you.'

'The same old Kate,' he said. 'Always got the hump.'

'So what's the confession Dad? Smacking me and Mum around? I know all about that already.'

He was suddenly serious. 'No love. Worse than that.' He hesitated. 'Listen. I know I've been a bad man all my life. Despicable. But now I'm going to meet my maker and I need to make recompense.'

'How?' she asked.

'I want to tell you a story. I need to get this off my chest with one of the family.'

'And you've chosen me,' she interrupted.

'Right.'

'I don't think I want to hear.'

'It's up to you. I know you think badly of me, and this will only make it worse. But I loved you Kate, and still do. Whatever happened between us. And I think you're the only one I want to know about something I did. I don't know why, but I do. Listen, there's a bottle of scotch in the cupboard over there. Wrapped up in a towel. Get it for us will you.'

'You've got cirrhosis.'

'Too late to worry about that now. You got any fags? Those buggers won't let me smoke, none of them.'

'They'll kill you. That and the booze.'

'The way you feel, you'll probably be glad.'

'Maybe.'

'Who gives a monkey's? Not me. I'm too far gone for that. Go on gel, do your old man a last favour.'

She looked at the old geezer in the bed. A faint shadow of what he had been, and felt a momentary pang of pity, although she didn't want to. She suddenly thought of being woken in the middle of the night when Johnny had been working and came home with presents for her and Dolly.

Expensive stuff. Toys and games and books for Kate, perfume and fancy clothes for Dolly. She remembered being allowed to get up all sleepy-headed and seeing her mum and dad dancing in the front room to some old Elvis record, and tears filled her eyes. 'All right Dad,' she said. 'Just this once. Got a glass and something to use for an ashtray?'

39

'Now listen Kate,' he said when they were both lit up, plastic beakers of scotch in their hands. 'I know I ain't got long. My liver's fucked, and I'm living on borrowed time. But there's something I've got to tell you.'

'I don't know that I want to hear.'

'Maybe not. But I need you to. Before I tell you, come here, let me have a look at you. It's been too long.'

She did as he asked, smelling death on his breath.

He peered closely at her face. 'What's that?' he said. 'A bruise. How'd you get that?'

'Have a guess,' she replied. 'Robbo's like you

were.'

'He hits you?'

'What do you think?'

'Christ, I'd like to get my hands on him.'

'Now *you're* the one getting righteous,' she said, pulling back. 'You gave enough bruises to me and Mum in your time.'

'And I'm ashamed.'

'Sure.'

'I mean it. I'm sorry.'

'Too late for that Dad,' she said. 'Far too late.'

'It's never too late to ask for forgiveness Kate. I've learnt that. And I want you to forgive me.'

'Can't be done Dad.'

'I'm sorry you feel that way. But there's something else. Something I haven't even told the priest.'

'What?'

'I killed some people.'

'Quite a few if what I've heard is right.'

'No, you don't get it. I've *had* people killed. People who took liberties with me and mine. They knew what they were doing and took a chance. I'm talking about me personally killing people. Innocent people really. In cold blood.'

'What are you talking about Dad?' she asked, suddenly chilled in the overheated room. She didn't want to hear. Just wanted to go home.

He sensed her discomfort and gripped the sleeve of her jacket with some of his old strength. 'Kids,' he said. 'Years ago. You remember the college boys shot to death in a motor down Southend way?'

'What? When?'

'February 2000. It was in all the papers. They never got anyone.'

Kate vaguely remembered seeing the TV news one lunchtime when she was waiting for *Neighbours* to come on, seeing coppers standing round uselessly, their breath steaming in the freezing air whilst a tarpaulined car was put on a low loader. 'I remember, I think,' she said.

'Shotgunned,' he said, staring off into space. 'All three blown to bits. No motive. No one knew what they were doing there. But I do.'

'What?'

'They were university boys studying chemistry. Then they decided to do a bit of chemistry of their own. Making E tablets. And good ones too. Pure MDMA. Or at least as pure as you could get them days. They had a right little factory going inside the uni. Perfect it was. They came to one of the clubs I was at, and we did a deal, and they sold the stuff to us wholesale. It was a dream. Then a couple of the bouncers got greedy and decided to get in on the act. Upped the price a bit, and thought they could cut me out. They made a meet down some country lane, but some soppy bird one of them was shagging got wind of it, got pissed, and opened her stupid mouth too wide.'

'What happened to them?' asked Kate.

'We tuned them up a bit in the cellar, and they spilled the beans. They ain't so tough them bouncers. All mouth and no trousers, most of them. So me and a few of the boys turned up instead. We had shooters, and it all got a bit silly.'

'You killed them.'

'One of them had a shooter himself, and started waving it about.'

'And?'

'One of the chaps I was with. Freddie the Fish. Remember him?'

'Vaguely.'

'He had a pump action. Starts blasting away, and we all got involved. I didn't want to, but we'd had a few toots. You know how it is.'

'Not really.' Kate thought of the gun she'd been handling herself not so long ago, and felt even colder at the thought of what could be done with it.

'Take my word for it. Normally I wouldn't have gone, but we were a bit short-handed. It was a fucking replica anyway, as it goes. The gun the kid had. Stupid little prick.'

'So why are you telling me?'

'I need absolution.'

'From me?'

He nodded.

'No it's not about me. It's all about you as usual. Spreading more grief. As if you haven't done enough.'

'Don't be like that babe.'

'Don't fucking babe me. My life's shit enough as it is, without you giving me more.'

'I'm truly sorry,' said Johnny.

'Take your sorry and stick it up your arse.' And with that Kate left the room, went downstairs and out to her car without speaking to Ben. She drove a quarter of a mile or so and pulled into a space, where she sat and cried until there were no more tears to come.

Johnny died a week later. When Ben called to tell her, she put down the phone on him without a word.

The funeral was a week later. Kate hadn't wanted to go but Robbo insisted. 'You've got to,' he said. 'Show respect.'

'I don't respect that old bastard. Never did.'

'Have a heart. Anyway, how would it look if you didn't go?'

'Couldn't care less. You want to go so bad, go on your own,' she said.

Robbo back-handed her almost casually. 'Enough of your fuckin' lip, girl.'

My girl, thought Kate as she backed away from him. That's just what my dad called mum, you bastard. 'All right,' she said. 'if it means so much to you.' Anything to avoid yet another smack.

'Got to show our faces,' said Robbo. 'Do the right thing.'

The day of the funeral dawned bright. Ben had made all the arrangements with the other brothers, as Kate had positively refused to have anything to do with it. The entourage kicked off from the house in Plaistow. Black horses pulled the hearse, followed by at least a dozen black limos carrying the cream of East London villainy. Kate and Robbo were in the third motor with brother Keith and his wife, a right nasty little slag from Kennington who reckoned she was worth a lot more than she was. Kate hated her. In fact she detested all her brother's wives. They thought much the same way about her and she couldn't have cared less. In front of the hearse were a couple of fake gangsters on motorbikes who somehow always managed to turn up at villain's funerals, between writing books about their imaginary exploits and appearing in reality TV shows.

Kate stared out of the car's tinted glass at the crowds lining the route to the cemetery where Johnny was going to be buried next to Dolly's grave. 'What stone do these ghouls crawl out from under?' she asked no one in particular.

Everyone was silent aside from Keith's wife, who said with fake sincerity, 'Johnny would be proud that so many people loved him.'

'Loved him,' said Kate. 'Terrified of him more like.'

'No Kate,' said Keith. 'He changed.'

'Sure he did,' said Kate. Fucking old hypocrite, she thought. I hope he rots in hell.

After the ceremony it was all back to the house again where caterers had laid on a lavish buffet spread and the champagne corks began to pop.

'It's what the old man would've wanted,' said Ben in his speech at the wake as tears rolled down his face.

In fact there was hardly a dry eye in the place apart from Kate's, as people became maudlin with too much drink.

'I've got to go,' she said to her husband. 'I can't stand any more of this.'

'Bollocks,' said Robbo. 'It's just starting to get lively.'

'Then you stay,' she said. 'I'll get a cab home.'

'Please yourself,' he said, and moved deeper into the house where he thought a few old mates were cutting out lines of coke.

Fuck you then, thought Kate, and phoned a cab company on a card stuck to the notice board in the kitchen. Fuck the lot of you.

40

And still there was no definite date for the robbery. The reason for the delay was that Deep Throat had been waiting for a big pay day, and it was just round the corner. Some months the pickings were lean, others bountiful. It made sense. At Christmas and during the summer holidays there was a lot of dirty cash about, never mind credit cards and chip and pin. Other times people kept their hands in their pockets and their money clean. So that particular month, when the kids were out of school, he knew that there would be a bumper bundle heading for destruction. Exactly how much he wouldn't know until closer to the time. The exact amount was crucial. He was on a nice little earner if all went well. Now his two daughters were growing up it was harder and harder to make ends meet on his salary. And the girls were of prime importance. Three, if you counted his wife, which in fact he hardly did. They'd been married a long time, and the shine was long gone. But she cared for the family, which was what counted most, and left him pretty well to get on with his own devices. All in all, a pretty tidy arrangement. If only he could kick his one bad habit.

The first geezer who'd approached him, a bald-headed bloke who could frighten little children with one look, had made that clear. Deep Throat had a little problem with the gee-gees. That was the trouble really, and he'd had a bad run a few months earlier. His bookie who was not strictly kosher, had sold the debt on to baldie who'd introduced himself as Mister Stone, although Deep Throat was willing to bet that was not his real name. Willing to bet, that was grimly ironic, as it was betting that had got him into this bad position.

Mister Stone had buttonholed him in his local one Saturday afternoon as he was watching his money go down the pan during a steward's enquiry. 'No good?' the bald man said.

'No good at all,' said Deep Throat. 'That fucking jockey should be shot. Balked. I'd balk the bastard.'

'Bad luck.'

'Yeah…'

'Still, better luck next time,' said the bald man.

'Cheers. I had a good tip, on the one o'clock, but that turned out to be another donkey.'

'Aren't they all where you're concerned?'

'Do what?'

'The nags. Seems like you've had a bad run, and you owe me.'

'I don't know what you're on about,' and Deep Throat made to get up. But Stone was too fast for him and gripped his wrist hard.

'Don't walk away from me mate,' he said. 'Or your wife and daughters will suffer.'

Deep Throat felt the sweat break out of every pore, and he almost wet his pants. 'What do you mean?' Stone still had his fingers tightly wrapped round Deep Throat's wrist.

'According to the figures I've been given, you owe close to two grand to a mate of mine.' He mentioned the bookie's name and Deep Throat knew that his worst nightmares were coming true. 'He's tired of chasing you round,' Stone went on in a conversational tone, as if they were just two friends discussing the favourite for the next race. 'Now, he could inform your employers, who I believe take a dim view of such goings on. Or. He could let me buy the debt off him and collect from you myself. And that's what he's done. He's knocking on a bit, and doesn't need the aggro. So I gave him half the money, and now you owe me.'

'I was going to pay.'

'Course you were. But there's ways and means.'

'What do you mean?'

'Got the money on you?'

'Course not.'

'Hole in the wall?'

'I'm overdrawn.'

'It's not good mate is it? I could break your fucking legs. Or I could see to it that those daughters of yours learn how hard the world is when daddy doesn't pay his debts.'

'No.' Deep Throat went to get up again, but one look from Stone kept him pinned to his seat.

'Or I could make you a rich man.'

'How?'

'That place you work at. The bank. I'd like to make a withdrawal.'

Deep Throat knew then that he was in deep trouble. 'I need the toilet,' he said.

'Go on then,' said Stone. 'But don't think about doing a runner. I know where you live. And more importantly, where your girls live.'

So that was the start of it. When he returned from the lavatory where he'd lost his lunch, Stone bought Deep Throat a drink and told him what he knew about the money run, which was quite a lot.

He'd done his research.

Deep Throat's first instinct was to go to the police after Stone left. Tell them everything and let them sort it out. There might be a reward from the bank, and that would help. But when he left the pub he found a white envelope with his name on it neatly tucked under one windscreen wiper on his car. Inside was a photo of his wife and daughters outside his front door. They were probably on the way to school. On the back of the photo was written neatly: 'JUST IN CASE YOU GET ANY IDEAS'.

That put the kibosh on that idea.

Over the next weeks Deep Throat and Stone met often. He wasn't a bad bloke really, and never mentioned the debt again. In fact he'd often drop Deep Throat a few quid to put on a horse.

So, slowly Deep Throat got used to the idea. A cut of the cash was his when the money was disposed of. Of course Stone could be lying, but somehow he trusted the man. Old school armed robber that he was, it would be easier to cough up than leave Deep Throat out in the cold, ready to blow the whistle.

Of course he knew that someone might get hurt. But that was the way life was. People were always getting hurt. Just look at the papers. Wars, hurricanes, landslips, tsunamis. Every day he read about some disaster, natural or man-made. And he couldn't let anything happen to the girls. Even if it meant him going to jail, which was obviously another option.

Then one day Stone told him he might not be round for a bit. Deep Throat felt a swell of relief until Stone told him another man would be in touch. 'You think I'm bad,' said Stone. 'I'm a pussycat compared to this bloke.'

And that's when Connie entered Deep Throat's life.

41

Of course the big question was how to get the money wagon somewhere where the gang could open up the back without causing too much of a fuss. No one wanted a shoot-out on the highway. Too messy. So when Deep Throat gave a day, time and route for the cash to Connie, he also gave up the names of the two crew who'd be on board.

Their names were Jim and Ken. Jim was the driver, the key man. He was in his twenties, married with a baby and lived just a short hop from the depot. He was nothing special, just a bloke doing a job for wages. He might just as well have been driving baked beans around. He'd been employed for two years and had a clean sheet. No obvious vices, which was perfect.

Ken was older. Ex-army, which could be a problem. But then problems were made to be solved.

As per Eddie's plan, Connie sent in the enforcers on the day of the robbery.

There were two of them. John Knowles, known as Knocker, because that's what he liked to do. Knock people out. His boyfriend was Charlie Simms. They were both as gay as tangerines, and lived together in a chi-chi apartment in Brixton. They were both actors and stuntmen. And thieves. Because acting and stunt work didn't pay enough to support their rather extravagant lifestyle, and because Charlie fancied himself as something of a make-up artist, they were perfect. Made for the job. They'd done background for dozens of TV shows. They'd been in *The Bill*, *Silent Witness*, *Trial and Retribution*, and loads more. But not only TV work. They'd also been in several feature films, they'd proudly tell anyone who'd listen. Check out *Essex Boys*, blink and you'd miss Knocker. Put on a DVD of *Gangster No1*, and there's Charlie for a few seconds. You see both their specialities were playing coppers, which was a joke, as they both had long records. But the advantage was they knew how to play the part, and in fact both had their own police uniforms, which they'd put together from theatrical agencies and what they could purloin on set.

When Connie cornered them one morning in a cafe in Kennington where they were enjoying breakfast and checking out the price of a new HD-TV from Dixons in *The Sun*, they jumped at his offer. Twenty-five grand, up front, just to babysit a woman and kid for a few hours. You certainly didn't make that sort of money for a day's work on *Waking the Dead* for BBC1.

And that was the plan. Knocker and Charlie would turn up at Jim's door early on the morning of the raid. They'd be togged up in the uniforms, and Charlie would have made them up to look as different as possible without it being too obvious. They'd have some story to get them inside, or worst case scenario, they'd just push their way in, loaded guns in their hands, and Jim would be left with no option but to do exactly what he was told or else. Connie knew they'd have no compunction about getting a bit fisty with the missus if Jim put up any objections.

Then it was up to him to convince his mate that discretion was the better part of valour and give up the truck without a fight. Of course it was risky. But then so much in life was. Jim could inform the cops and they could go in guns blazing. But then it was Knocker and Charlie's job to let him know what could happen to mother and baby if that happened. Bad things. Very bad things.

Of course the rest of the gang would be armed that morning and if they had to do the business, so be it. This was the biggun' according to Deep Throat. Twenty million. Ten million for the chaps after the money exchange was made. And then they'd all be sitting pretty on a mountain of cash.

42

Whilst the plans were being formulated, Ali was feeding Kate information about the gang's master plan to get rid of the dodgy cash and replace it with brand-new. And Kate was constantly in touch with Sadie. They'd meet at various locations around East London and Essex, and compare notes.

'I knew it would be me and you girl,' said Sadie, one sunny afternoon in the coffee shop of a book-store in Beckton. 'So how's it going?'

'Crap,' said Kate. 'I know it's going to be soon, Robbo's getting amorous all of a sudden.'

'Is that right. And how about Ali?'

'He wants it all the time too. I'm fucking exhausted.'

'Lucky girl. I haven't had a decent shag in ages.'

'No. You're the lucky one. Ali's changed since he's been with that lot. He used to be sweet. Now it's wham, bam, thank you ma'am. And he wants to do it up my… you know.'

'Your arse, sweetheart? All men want that sooner or later. But he's still keen?'

'Keener than ever. But different.'

'It'll be the company he's keeping,' Sadie said, consolingly.

'Probably.'

'Maybe Poppy and Nik have got the right idea.'

'What? Go the other way?'

'Could be,' said Kate.

'Nah. I like cock. And when this is all over, and we've got right away, I intend to have my share.'

'You're welcome to both of mine.'

'A Paki and a wife-beater. No thanks.' She saw the look on Kate's face. 'Sorry love.'

'That's all right. It'll be worth it in the end. So where are you going?'

'It's bad luck to talk about it.'

'You reckon?'

'Whatever. Somewhere hot, with no extradition. Or cops you can buy off.'

'Sounds perfect.'

'You're welcome to come along.'

'I might just do that. What about passports?'

'I was going to talk to you about that. I know a bloke. Well, a mate of Eddie's really.'

'Aren't they all?'

'Too true. He'll do the business for a grand. Good work too.'

'What does he need?'

'Apart from the money? Just a name, date of birth, and a photo.'

'You got the money?'

'Yeah. Had to pop a bit of tom. But I managed.'

'I'm up for it.'

'Right. But I'll need cash up front. Sorry, love. In the old days, you know... But those days have gone.'

'Have there been any offers on the house yet?'

'A couple.'

'Any good?'

'Yes and no. I'm giving the estate agent one too, you know. String everything along.'

'I thought you hadn't had sex.'

'I said a *good* shag, Katie. This sod only lasts a few seconds before he shoots his load.'

'You're mental.'

'I try love. I try,' said Sadie, with a mischievous look on her face.

So the days passed until Deep Throat gave the

final word, which, like the love-struck man he was, Ali passed on to Kate. Everything was arranged. Everything was arranged. Now all they could do was wait.

43

And finally it arrived. A perfect day for a white wedding, or for that matter, a big knock off. Cool, cloudy, and dry. Knocker and Charlie parked a plain blue saloon, stolen the previous day, and fitted with new number plates, in the next street to Jim Flynn's house. Charlie had disguised them both before leaving home, which they did wearing long anoraks over their uniforms. Nothing spectacular. No false beards or moustaches. Just a little face padding here and there, coloured contacts, and hair dye. Both agreed that even their mothers, God rest their souls, would have trouble identifying them, especially with the police hats on. In their pockets they had balaclavas to wear once inside the house. They adjusted their uniforms as they left the car, high visibility jackets on, and fake radios on their lapels. Inside the jackets they both wore side arms in shoulder holsters.

They walked together into Flynn's street, both aware that all sorts of things could go wrong. A nosy neighbour could spot them and wonder why they didn't leave the house. Christ, anything. But that new TV and a granite worktop kitchen beckoned. The street was quiet in the early morning light, not a curtain twitched and the pavement was deserted. Luck was with them.

Knocker rapped on the door and rang the bell. Minutes later a dishevelled looking Jim Flynn, in pyjamas and dressing gown answered. 'Mr Flynn,' said Charlie.

'Yes. What is it?' He was as sleepy and surprised as they'd expected.

'It's about your mother.' Deep Throat knew that Jim's mum was an invalid, living alone.

'Christ. What's happened to her?' said Jim, blood rushing from his face.

'Can we come in?' asked Knocker.

'Sure. My God. Is she all right?'

They passed through the door and Jim closed it behind them.

'Tell me,' he said.

'Your mother's fine,' said Knocker, drawing his

pistol, and pushing Jim up against the wall. 'It's your wife and kid you've got to worry about.'

Jim didn't have a clue what was going on.

'Where are they?' demanded Charlie, pulling out his balaclava, taking off his cap, and pulling it on over his head, as Knocker held his gun on Jim.

'In bed. What is this?'

'You'll find out,' said Knocker, aping Charlie's move with his woolly disguise.

'Who is it Jim?' came a female voice from upstairs.

'Tell her to come down, on her own,' said Charlie, his voice muffled.

'Come down Sue,' said Jim. 'Leave the baby.'

'What is it?'

'Just come down.'

They heard movement from upstairs and a pretty young woman came down the steps belting up her dressing gown. She saw the uniforms, the guns and the balaclavas and stopped a few steps up. 'Is this a joke?' she said. 'Some of your mates from...'

'Be quiet Mrs Flynn,' said Knocker. 'This is no joke. Let's all sit down, and keep calm.'

She came into the hall and all four moved through the door on the left into a small lounge. 'Sit,' said Charlie.

'My baby,' said Sue. She made a move to rush

upstairs to the nursery, but was restrained by Charlie.

'Your baby will be fine,' he said calmly, releasing her shoulders from his grasp. 'You all will be, if everybody does what they're told.'

'The money,' said Jim, suddenly understanding.

'Ten out of ten,' said Charlie. 'Where's the kitchen Sue? I think we could all do with a nice cup of tea.'

44

———➤◦◄———

Charlie took Sue into the kitchen next door to the living room. It was small, with a window looking out over a tiny back yard. Charlie pulled down a blind and switched on the overhead light. She was shaking so hard he had to fill the kettle and switch it on for her. 'Just make us a pot of tea love,' he said. 'And all will be well. And don't get any bright ideas about throwing boiling water at me. Remember who's in the next room, and more importantly upstairs. It's only money. And as soon as Jim does the business for us, we'll be off, and you can get back to your life.'

They were interrupted by a baby's cry from above. 'It's his feed time,' said Sue.

'Right. We'll go and get junior, and I'll brew up whilst you fill his face.'

They went to the staircase and climbed the short flight. Upstairs were three doors. One to the parent's bedroom, one to a box room that had been turned into a nursery, and the third was open to a bathroom/toilet. 'Nice house,' said Charlie. 'Worth a bob or two I suppose.'

'To the building society,' said Sue, as she entered the nursery and picked a small child from a cot.

'He or she?' asked Charlie.

'I thought you'd know everything.'

'Not everything love. So?' Although he did. He just wanted to keep her talking. Keep her sweet.

'A boy. John.'

'Nice name.'

'You're not going to rape me are you?' asked the young woman.

Charlie laughed. As if. 'Sue,' he said. 'That's not why we're here. We're here to make some dough. Relax, and in a couple of hours we'll be gone.' He didn't tell her he was gay, and was more likely to rape her husband. That was one thing she didn't need to hear.

Downstairs again, the kettle has boiled and Charlie made four teas, clumsy in his gloves. The pistol was back in its holster. He was sure he had nothing to fear from the woman who was busy making up a bowl of breakfast for baby John. All in all thought Charlie, it was a most cosy, domestic scene.

He called the other two into the kitchen where Sue was sitting down, John on her lap, taking a spoon from the bowl to his mouth and back. They sat Jim down next to her and explained the plan.

'Smile Jim,' said Knocker. 'You go to work as usual. I know it's going to be hard, but you must act naturally. We don't want any harm coming to Sue and the baby.'

'John,' said Charlie.

'Sue and John,' Knocker went on. 'You take out the truck, and you tell Ken what's going on. Now Ken might want to play the hero. But if he does, we'll know, and you'll be going to a funeral. A double funeral.'

Sue almost dropped the baby and started shaking again.

'Relax Sue,' said Charlie. 'It ain't going to happen. Jim's going to make sure his mate knows that if we go down, someone will be calling at Ken's address just like we did this morning. But they won't be half as polite as us. No tea. Just a petrol bomb through the window in the middle of the night. OK, Jim?'

Jim nodded. 'If you hurt a hair on their heads…' he said, half rising from his chair.

'Don't be silly,' said Knocker, picking up the pistol he'd put on the drainer. 'You don't have to prove how brave you are Jim. Macho. We know you'll do anything to protect Sue and John. And you will. They'll come to no harm, promise. As long as you just be good and wait for someone to let you know what they want you to do. Couldn't be simpler. OK? And not one single word to anyone, especially the police.'

Jim nodded.

'Tell him Sue,' said Charlie. 'No coppers. Well, only us.'

'Do it Jim,' said Sue. 'Like the man said, it's only money.'

45

Knocker kept an eye on Jim as he got dressed for work, trying to keep him calm and focused whilst Charlie stayed downstairs with Sue and the baby. He sat at the kitchen table and made small talk, as Sue bustled around trying to make the day as normal as possible. But she was still shaky and dropped a cup into the sink where it smashed into a dozen pieces. 'Relax, love,' said Charlie. 'Just sit down and take it easy, and I'll make some more tea.'

When Jim and Knocker came downstairs, Jim gave Sue a big hug and kissed the baby. 'I'll see you later,' he said.

'Course you will,' said Charlie. 'Just keep that thought in mind.'

Knocker handed Jim a fully-charged, paid-up mobile phone, and said, 'Keep this close. You'll get instructions as you go along. Just do as you're told, and we'll be out of your hair.'

'I'm finished,' said Jim, almost in tears.

'Listen,' said Knocker. 'You'll be bloody famous by tonight. You and Sue'll be on *Richard and Judy* telling your story next week. Just focus, Jim. Keep a clear head and you'll be fine.'

'But why me?'

'Shit happens son, shit happens.'

Knocker watched from the window as Jim got into his car, sat for a moment, then started it and drove off. This is going to be the hard part - waiting, he thought.

Jim Flynn clenched the steering wheel tightly as he drove to the depot. His first thought was to call the police, but his second was the two huge, armed men sitting in his kitchen with his wife and child as if they'd just popped in for morning coffee. Oh God, don't let them be hurt, he thought, then steeled himself as he drove through the security gates and into the depot's yard.

He met Ken in the changing rooms, and the older man looked at him and said, 'You look rough son. What's up?'

Jim tried to put on a happy face. 'Take-out last night. Think I got a bad prawn. Been up all night.'

'Should've called in sick boy.'

'No. I'll be fine. Got the job sheet?'

'Yeah. A big consignment for burning. Wouldn't mind a bit of that. What about you?'

'Never think about it Ken.'

'Seems a shame to waste all that cash. Still, that's what they pay us for. Come on son, look lively. Time we weren't here.'

Jim changed into his olive green uniform, complete with safety vest, put on his hard helmet and joined Ken at the truck. It had already been loaded and sat low on its heavy duty suspension. Ken was busy checking the tyre pressure and Jim swung himself up into the driver's seat. Last time I'll do this, he thought. Whatever happens they'll never trust me with this job again. Suddenly he felt tears in his eyes again, but hardened his heart as Ken got into the passenger seat. 'I've got the route,' he said. 'We're going the pretty way.'

The foreman came over with a clipboard for the men to sign, and Jim's hand trembled as he did it.

He drove out of the depot, turned left, left again on to the main road, and joined the morning rush. 'Take the next left son,' said Ken, with the route map on his lap, and Jim obeyed.

'Oi,' said Ken suddenly, and Jim almost jumped out of his skin.

'What?'

'Where's your lunch son? You know I love Sue's sandwiches.'

'No time this morning. The nipper was playing up. I'll get something the other end.'

'I've got plenty. You can share mine,' said Ken. 'You know Dot always makes a bloody ton.'

Jim almost wept again, at his friend's kindness. His friend, who he was soon going to put in harm's way.

46

As they drove the prescribed route, Jim's stomach was clenching like a boxer's fist, and he felt that, at any moment his bowels might open and fill his pants. 'Ken,' he said.

'What's the matter?'

'We're being robbed.'

'Do what?'

'We're being robbed.'

'I don't get you son,' said Ken, looking round as if there was someone else in the cab of the truck besides them.

'Just listen,' said Jim. 'Two men came to my house this morning dressed as policemen.'

Ken was quick on the uptake. 'Oh fuck.'

'Yes. I'm sorry mate. But they've got Sue and the nipper. They've got guns.'

'Jesus, Jim. And you just left them there?'

'What could I do?'

'You could've called the Bill.'

'They said they'd kill 'em.'

'The money.'

'Course. It's a big load init?'

'Twenty mill, give or take.'

'What we going to do?'

'I'll call base.'

'Don't Ken. If anything happens to Sue and John…'

'We've got to.' Ken took out his mobile.

'Don't do it Ken. It's my family. I don't want to hurt you.'

Ken was army trained, although a bit past it. But the look he saw in the younger, weaker man's eyes told him that, friends or not, he'd fight him to the death before he allowed him to make the call. 'OK son. What's going to happen?' he said and shoved the phone back in his pocket.

'I'm going to get a call on this phone,' said Jim, one-handedly tugging out the mobile Knocker had given him. 'And I do whatever they say.'

'You know we're fucked if we do it.'

'I know mate. But what would you do?'

'Just what you're doing. We've been pals for a

long time Jim. I'll do whatever you say. But if I get a chance at 'em…'

'Yeah, I know mate.'

'When?'

'Whenever.'

'Then drive on, driver.'

And that was when the phone Jim was holding rang.

47

He fumbled, and almost dropped the instrument, and the truck swerved.

'Careful,' shouted Ken. 'You'll have us off the road.'

'Christ,' said Jim, straightening the wheel and at the same time pushing the green button to receive calls.

'Morning Jim,' said a voice in his ear. 'Hope I haven't caught you at a bad time.'

'Who are you?' demanded Jim.

'Now, now. None of that. Look in your mirror.'

Jim did so, and two cars back, main beams flashed. 'See us?' said the voice.

'Yes.'

'Good. Now we know you're GPS'd up, so this has to be quick. Take the next B road. It's coming up in about two minutes. Drive along until you come to a lay-by. It's about half a mile. It's been closed off. Pull up in there and leave the engine running. We'll be right behind you. Got it?'

'Got it.'

'And no funny business. Tell Ken as well. We'll be in and out in a few minutes, and Sue and John will be safe and sound. OK?'

Jim said nothing.

'Talk to me Jim,' said the voice.

'OK. But they'd better be or I'll hunt you to the ends of the earth.'

'No melodrama mate. We don't want to hurt them. Keep the phone on.'

Jim tossed it onto the dash with a clatter, and as ordered, slowed and pulled onto the B road that came up fast. He drove down until he saw a lay-by on the left. The entrance was blocked by cones, and a no entry sign. There was a man standing by it, shovel in hand, wearing a baseball cap and a scarf over the lower part of his face, with sunglasses over his eyes. When he saw the truck he hastily pulled the cones apart to allow access for it and the following car. As soon as they were inside, he replaced the cones and vanished into the wooded copse on the far side of the lay-by. Jim pulled up and left the engine running as ordered as the car drove up tight behind him and two huge, masked armed men got out. Jim heard a voice from the phone and picked it up. 'Right Jim,' said the voice which he assumed to be from the leader of the gang. 'On your left at the end is an opening. Drive straight through. It's tight, but you can do it. Don't worry about the paintwork, I'm sure it's insured.'

Jim looked at the scrub and trees at the side of the lay by. As usual the area was full of cans and paper and general rubbish, and sure enough at the end was enough space to take the truck. He put it into gear, bumped up the kerb, if it could be called that and into the wood. The undergrowth scraped the side of the truck and the going was rough but do-able. Suddenly the wood opened up into a field where two bright yellow JCB earth moving machines were parked with exhaust puffing into the air. Next to the JCB's was a large white two ton truck with its number plate covered with a white rag 'Stop,' said the voice in Jim's ear, as the two masked men broke through the undergrowth behind them, guns at the ready. The leader was still talking into the phone. 'Out you get chaps,' said the voice. 'And be cool.'

'He wants us out,' said Jim.

'Shit,' said Ken. 'This sort of thing happened in

Northern Ireland when I was there.'

'And?'

'Usually someone died.'

'Come on now, the pair of you.' said the voice. 'We don't have all day.'

Jim and Ken unlocked the truck and climbed out. The two men pushed them to the side of the truck. 'Blindfold time chaps,' said the leader who now switched the phone off and dropped it the pocket of the Barbour jacket he was wearing. 'Don't want you seeing too much.'

'No,' said Ken with panic in his voice. 'That what the bloody Provos did, then shot my mates,' and he lunged at the leader who chopped him down with a vicious blow to the head. 'Unnecessary,' he said to Ken's still form. 'We ain't killers.'

He knelt down, felt Ken's pulse, and nodded. 'He'll be all right,' he said. 'Bit of a headache. That's all.' But blindfolded him nevertheless and fastened his wrists and ankles with plastic ties. 'Your turn Jim. Don't worry.'

Jim allowed himself to be blindfolded and tied too, after he'd lain down next to his mate. When the two were secure, the leader made a gesture with his gun hand, and the two JCB's lurched forward. Both the drivers were also masked. The two huge machines slowly took up position, one at the front of the money truck with its shovel hard against the bonnet, and the second swung round and smashed into the rear doors. The metal buckled but held as the truck's alarm screamed. Another blow, another screech of metal and the truck broadsided. The first JCB moved in harder, and the second struck for the third time, and the doors began to cave in. One more hit and the doors flew open, exposing the metal cages packed with black plastic sacks labelled 'PROPERTY OF HM TREASURY.' The driver of the front JCB jumped out, dived into the two-tonner and drove it closer to the weighty piles of cash. The three men frantically began to transfer the money, whilst the leader kept an eye on *his* prisoners. When the loading was almost complete, he took out the phone again, pressed a pre-programmed number and said, 'All right? No probs? Sweet. Same here. All done. You can go home now.' He killed the phone and said to Jim. 'That was your place Jim. Wife and child doing well.'

'Thank you,' said Jim.

'Don't mention it,' said the leader, then shouted, 'Come on you lot. Chop, chop.'

As Jim lay he heard the sound of liquid being poured, then twin *whoomps* as the JCB's were torched, then the truck's engine started and it moved away, then in the distance the sound of a car starting, then nothing, apart from the alarm and the roar of the flames destroying the JCBs, and he began to desperately tug at the cuffs around his wrists.

The robbery had happened as planned. Result.

48

Connie, Joe and Robbo had left for the job late the previous evening, telling their wives that they were off for a game of high stakes poker, and not to expect them back until they arrived, and under no circumstances to call them on their mobiles, as they'd be switched off. Niki, Poppy and Kate meekly accepted their lies, kissed them on their cheeks, wished them the best of luck in the game, and straight away hit the phones.

The plan was for the girls to get a good night's sleep, then early the next morning Poppy would drive to Niki's, pick her up, then on to Kate's, pick her up too, and finally drive to Sadie's to pick up their weapons and prepare for battle. But no one had much sleep that night. As soon as the men had left, Poppy went straight to Niki's and they spent the night together in her bed. The first time they had ever met at one another's house.

'This feels weird,' said Poppy, after they had made love and were lying together in the dark.

'What? Being in my bed?' said Niki.

'Being in his bed.'

'After tomorrow it won't matter. It'll be no one's bed. I might set fire to it before we leave.'

'I'm scared Niki. What happens if it all goes wrong?'

'It won't.'

'You can't be sure. The guns and everything. They might not even get the money.'

'They will.'

'But what happens if something happens to one of us?'

'Don't think about it sweetheart. I'll protect you. I'd die for you.'

'That's what I'm afraid of.'

'I'm a Cossack, Poppy. I'm bullet proof.'

'God, I hope so.'

'Trust me.'

'I do,' said Poppy as she kissed her lover. 'I do.'

At her house Kate sat up alone, her stomach churning as she thought of what tomorrow would bring. And as for Sadie, she sat alone too, loading and unloading the weapons that sat on the floor in front of her. Filling the magazines with bullets, then flicking them out and watching them bounce on the carpet. She was surrounded by the kit the women were going to wear the next day. Black jeans, black T-shirts, black hoodies, and each of the girls had bought their own black DM's.

If this goes pear-shaped, she thought, we're fucked good and proper. But who cares? At least we've done something for ourselves for once. She was proud of her little firm. Gangsters' wives one and all, and if it all goes down the tubes, she thought, at least we did our best. And no one can ask for better than that. She loved the other women. Once, she knew she would only have thought about herself. But now, the other three and her were closer than family. At least I got that out of all the shit that's happened, she thought, and as she gathered up a handful of slugs, she laughed out loud.

49

—————◦·◦·◦—————

The venue for the exchange of old money for new was an abandoned warehouse in Stratford just off the A12. The area was falling apart and just waiting for the bulldozers, when, all being well, a shiny new mini-city would be built in time for the 2012 Olympics, and everyone would make a nice few quid. The building itself had been half burnt out a couple of years before. The steel girders that made up its frame were rusty under a coating of soot and bird droppings from the pigeons that had taken up residence there. A high metal fence, covered in graffitied signs telling of the danger within to anyone foolish enough to enter, was hung with lethal razor wire, and the only entrance was a pair of wooden doors fastened with a padlock and chain.

It was late afternoon and the sun was beginning to sink behind the tower blocks that dominated the horizon.

Robbo used his mobile, and a minute later a man in an anorak appeared from the darkness of the building, undid the lock, slid the chain through, and pulled the doors open with a screech of wood on concrete.

Ali drove through the gates and the man pushed them to behind them.

Ali bounced the truck over the uneven tarmac inside and into the building proper which was a mixture of darkness and bright light where the holes in the roof allowed the bright rays of sunshine to enter. Anorak gestured for him to keep going in the direction of a dark blue truck parked with its sidelights on. Standing by it were three men. One was in a suit, the other two in leathers and jeans. Both of them were carrying Skorpion sub-machine guns.

Anorak signalled for Ali to drive close to the group and he did so and stopped the engine. One of the gunmen reached inside the driver's door of the blue van, and its main beams lit up the warehouse.

'Here goes nothing,' said Ali.

Ali, Connie, Robbo and Joseph exited the truck and Robbo said, 'There's no need for the weapons.'

'I'll be the judge of that Robbo,' said the suited man.

'Fair enough.'

'You got the dough?' asked The Suit.

'Every note,' said Connie in reply.

'You armed?' said The Suit again.

'Of course.'

'Right. That's why we are. So let's not get silly. All is well?'

'You got *our* cash?' said Joseph.

'Every note.'

'Then we're all friends here,' said Ali.

'Right,' said The Suit and gestured for his men to lower their guns, which they did.

'Let's have a squint then,' said Suit. 'And get this over and done with.'

Ali opened the back of the truck and exposed the money which was still neatly bagged. Suit waved Anorak over and he pulled out a black sack at random, split it with a flick knife he pulled from one of his pockets, and the bags inside spilled out onto the ground. 'Five thousand per bag, twenty bags to a sack,' he said. 'Nice of them to make it an easy count.'

'Hundred thousand a sack,' said The Suit. 'Right chaps, this is where we trust the pro's. But we all know what'll happen if there's been any messing about.'

'It's all there,' said Connie. 'Now where's ours?'

Anorak went to the back of the parked van and opened its doors to reveal ten large anonymous suitcases. 'A million quid in Euros in each,' he said. 'Non-consecutive. Pick a box.'

Connie tugged one of the suitcases out and opened the clasps. Inside were bricked, clean Euro notes, all colours of the rainbow. 'Fair enough,' he said. 'Now it's our turn to trust the pro's. But we all know what'll happen if there's been any messing about.'

For the first time The Suit smiled. 'Trust,' he said. 'A beautiful word.'

The men with the Skorpions slung them over their shoulders and together with Anorak started unloading the gangster's truck, now and then splitting a sack to check its contents. 'Just a precaution,' said Suit.

'I'd do just the same,' said Robbo.

'You're all over the news,' said Suit conversationally. 'Famous. Not the biggest cash robbery in history, but not bad. Just over twenty million they said.'

'That's what we make it,' said Connie as he yanked the suitcases out of the van and hauled them into their truck. 'But you can have the extra as a gift. Some of it'll be rotten I expect.'

'Oh, don't worry about that,' said Suit. 'Our smurfs are pretty good at getting rid of dirty money.'

When the exchange was over, the four men got into the van. Suit rolled down his window. 'Off on holiday now, are you?' he asked. 'Somewhere warm?'

'Could be,' said Connie.

'Yeah,' said Suit. 'I would. It's pretty warm round here at the moment. There's cops every-where. I'd make myself scarce if I was you lot.'

'We'll be OK,' said Connie.

'Well keep cool,' said Suit. 'We won't be in touch again. All being well that is.'

'All *is* well,' said Joseph.

'Be lucky then.'

'You too,' and the van lurched away in the direc-tion of the gate.

'Thank fuck for that,' said Robbo. 'Thought for a minute there we might be in trouble.'

50

'You are,' said a woman's voice from the darkness behind them. 'You all fucking are.' And Sadie, Poppy, Niki and Kate emerged into the light, all dressed in black and all carrying weapons which they trained on the men.

Connie was the first one to find his voice. 'Niki,' he said. 'What the fuck do you think you're doing love?'

'Pointing an Uzi subbie at you love,' she said. 'Fully loaded and set on auto. Now all of you take out your guns and throw them over there.' She gestured with the snub barrel of the gun she held to the darkest corner of the warehouse.

'You're having a fucking laugh,' said Robbo.

'Kate. Put that stupid gun down, or I'll knock you spark out.'

'Those days are over Robbo,' she replied. 'No more knocking me about. Now all of you, do what Niki said and lose your weapons.'

'Or what?' said Robbo. 'Just look at this cunt. She can't open a tin of beans without help, and here she is pointing a gun at us. Blimey, the noise'll make her cry. Fuck off love, you'll break a nail.'

'You didn't notice you prat, but my nails are gone. And as it happens I like the noise,' said Kate, and shot him in the thigh, the sound of the weapon sending the birds above into a frenzy of beating wings.

Robbo fell to the floor, a look of surprise on his face as he clutched at the wound which was spraying blood, the slug having gone in and out the other side. 'You fucking bitch. You shot me!' he said, unable to comprehend what was happening.

'Nice shooting Kate,' said Niki. 'I always said you were a natural.'

'Fucking help me,' said Robbo through gritted teeth.

'Do something for him,' said Sadie to Ali. 'You must know first-aid. But first, the guns, chaps.'

This time they all did as they were told. One by one, they pulled out their weapons and threw them into the corner. 'You too Robbo,' said Sadie, and he did the same.

'Ali,' said Kate. 'Do the business. Help him.'

Ali took off his belt and made a tourniquet for Robbo's thigh. 'How does he know first aid?' said Connie.

'Cos he's a fucking cozzer,' said Sadie. 'How do you think we knew where the meet was?'

'Do what?' demanded Connie. 'You Paki cunt.'

'Play nice boys,' said Sadie. 'Just let us have the money and we'll be off.'

'Off where?' said Joseph speaking for the first time. 'Poppy honey, what are you doing?'

'Don't honey me,' said Poppy. 'What were you going to do with your share? Send your bastard to Eton?'

'What bastard?' said Joseph, and Poppy lost it. She smashed him round the head with the barrel of her gun and he reeled away, head in hands as blood spurted from his nose.

'Leave it,' said Sadie, but it was too late. Poppy hit him again and again, the months of frustration and heartbreak at his betrayal finally finding an outlet.

Connie saw his chance. He wrenched the gun from Poppy's hand, turned it on the women, and fired. The bullet hit Poppy in the side, and she spun round from the force of it, a look of disbelief crossing her face as she tumbled slowly to the ground.

It was too much for Niki, seeing her lover lying there. She pulled the trigger on the Uzi and thirty nine millimetre slugs tore into Connie's body, opening up his chest and stomach so that the bloody contents spilled to the floor next to Poppy.

Niki ran to her friend's aid, as she lay bleeding on the floor, she threw down the empty gun, and pulled her trusty knife from its scabbard and looked at Joseph. 'You bastard,' she said, and lunged at him. But this time he was too quick and produced a small calibre pistol from the back of his belt and fired just as Niki pushed the blade deep into his chest. The sound of the shot was muffled by her body mass, and both hit the deck bleeding profusely, the gun clattering next to their bodies.

It had all happened so quickly there had been no time for Sadie, Kate or Ali to react, and as they stood there in the middle of the carnage and stink of blood and guts, Ali said, 'Christ, what do we do now?'

'Get the fuck out of here,' said Sadie. 'What else?'

'It wasn't supposed to be like this,' he said.

'That's life,' said Sadie, as she checked on Poppy and Niki. 'Or death. Depends how you look at it. Niki's dead, but Poppy's still breathing. We've got to get her out of here.'

'Will she be all right?' said Kate.

'Dunno,' replied Sadie, pulling off her hoodie and folding it, before pushing it over Poppy's wound to staunch the blood. 'How's Joseph?'

'Brown bread, the bastard,' replied Kate, as she tugged Niki's knife from Joseph's wound with a look of revulsion, wiped the blade on his jacket, then stuck it in her belt as she kicked his second gun out of sight.

'I'm going to kill you cunts,' said Robbo from where he was lying. 'Definite. You too Ali, you bastard. I should never have trusted you.'

'Don't be stupid,' said Kate. 'Or I'll kill you myself.'

Robbo was silent. He'd seen what she was capable of, and didn't want any more.

'And Ali,' said Kate.

'Yes.'

'Sorry love, but it's just me, Poppy and Sadie now.'

'What?'

'I've had enough of men. You're just another bloke Ali, just like Robbo except you don't smack me. All you wanted was to use me for information, well that, and for the sex. Shame for you that I'm good at more than just sucking cock.' She turned her gun on the Asian policeman. 'On the floor. You can keep Robbo company. You deserve each other. Now. Sadie, I'll drive.'

'Best idea I've heard all day,' said Sadie in reply.

And that's just what they did, taking Poppy with them, and gently putting her into the truck.

51

Kate jumped behind the wheel, whilst Sadie cared for Poppy who lay across the double passenger seat. The van screeched through the back streets towards the A12, wheels spinning and gears crashing. 'Slow down Kate,' Sadie yelled. 'You'll have old bill on us.'

'Sorry,' said Kate as she eased off the accelerator. 'Christ, that was bloody awful wasn't it.'

Sadie nodded, holding her hoodie onto Poppy's wound.

'How is she?' said Kate, taking her eyes off the road for a moment.

'She's breathing and her pulse is strong,' replied Sadie. 'I think she's going to be all right.'

'Christ, I hope so. Is the bullet still inside her?'

'No, it went right through. That's why there's so much blood.'

'Are they huge holes?'

'No. The one at the back's a bit bigger. Lucky it was only a small gun. And I think our Poppy has put on a bit of weight round the middle. I think it's just a flesh wound.'

'Then why won't she wake up?'

'Shock I think. I don't know Kate, I ain't a nurse.'

'You're doing a good job though.'

'I'm doing my best. That fucking Joseph. He got what he deserved.'

Kate nodded. 'What are we going to do? We can't take her to hospital can we?'

'No. We'd have to dump her, and she doesn't deserve that.'

'What then?'

'I know a bloke. A mate of Eddie's.'

'He would be.'

'Yeah, I know. Struck-off doctor. He'll fix her up.'

'You think he can make her better?'

'Course he can. He's done it enough times. It's where all the chaps go when they've had a bit of trouble. Bet your dad knew him.'

'Probably,' Kate replied as she swung onto the three-lane section of the A12 heading towards the Blackwall tunnel. 'Is this right,' she asked as she slid the truck into the middle lane. 'Where are we going? Is it far?'

'Not far,' replied Sadie. 'East Ham. Down the High Road. He's got a place above Iceland.'

'Will he be there?'

'He's always there love. Agoraphobic.'

'Jesus.'

'Yeah, I know. Get on the inside and take the A13.'

Dutifully Kate did as she was told and took the slip road and headed east. 'What are we going to tell Poppy about Nik?' she asked as they neared East Ham.

'The truth, what else? She died getting revenge.'

'That was our Niki all right. Then what? If Poppy gets better?'

'When she gets better, you mean,' said Sadie.

'That's what I meant. Sorry.'

'S'alright. Look, we've got loads of dough. We can find somewhere to hide out until Poppy can travel, then we're off, right. Like we said. Somewhere warm and safe. We've all got new passports, and she's on her own now. But she won't be. She'll have us. We're fucking family now Kate. Remember that.'

Kate nodded again, and Sadie relaxed the pressure for a moment and found cigarettes in her pocket. 'Want one?' she asked.

'Better not,' said Kate, slowing as she turned on to East Ham High Street.

'Why not. You smoke like a chimney.'

'Not any more.'

'Why not?'

'Well, as it goes Sade, there's something I need to tell you. I'm pregnant.'

'For Christ's sake. Are you kidding?'

'No.'

'So, who's the daddy?'

'Dunno. Like I told you, Robbo's been amorous recently and so has Ali.'

'Well, we'll know when it pops out. You are keeping it?'

'Course.'

'Cos this bloke does a nice line in abortions too from what I've heard.'

'Shut up.'

'Sorry love. But what a turn-up.'

'I know. I was so scared about getting hurt today.'

'So we really are a family. Christ, who would've thought it. You, pregnant. That's the place,' said Sadie suddenly. 'Iceland, see. Park up.'

'What are you going to do?'

'Go and knock on his door of course.'

'What happens if he says no?'

'I'll take this gun I've got in my pocket, stick it up

his arse and blow his brains out.'

'You're covered in blood Sade,' said Kate. 'Want me to go?'

'No. He don't know you. Give us your jumper.' She peeled off her blood soaked gloves and dropped them on the floor, then took Kate's hoodie and pulled it over her stained T-shirt. 'Don't show too much on my trousers does it?' she asked.

'No. they're black. No one notices anything anyway.'

'OK, wait here and I'll find the good doctor. Keep holding my hoodie on Poppy. Keep the pressure on.'

'OK. Hurry up. We don't want to lose Poppy, too.'

Sadie hopped out of the truck, and Kate held the garment on Poppy's side, applying firm pressure to staunch the blood flow. A moment later Poppy groaned and opened her eyes. 'Thank God,' said Kate. 'Poppy darlin' are you OK?'

'Oh Jesus, I hurt,' the girl replied. 'Where am I? What happened?'

'You got shot.'

'Is it bad?'

'Sadie says no. We're getting you seen to.'

'Hospital?' Poppy cried.

'No. Some geezer Eddie knows. He was a doctor. Is a doctor, I mean. You'll be fine.'

'Where's Niki? I need Niki,' said Poppy, plaintively.

Kate held Poppy's hand. 'Oh Poppy,' she said. 'Niki's not here. She got hurt.'

'Where is she then? In the back?' For the first time Poppy seemed to notice where she was.

'No love. She didn't make it. She died saving you.'

'Who did it? Who shot me? Who killed Niki?'

'Joseph. Then Niki killed him. With that knife. I got it for you.'

Poppy started to weep.

'Don't take on love, she loved you. She protected you right to the end.'

'Oh God, I wish it was me.'

'Don't say that. You don't mean it,' and Kate took Poppy gently in her arms and kissed her hair. 'We're here now. Me and Sade. We'll take care of you, I promise.'

Poppy just cried harder.

Once across the road Sadie body-swerved through the pedestrian traffic and rang the doorbell of the flat above the shop. There was no answer, so she rang again, and hammered hard on the wood with her fist. After what seemed like forever she heard shuffling footsteps from inside and the door opened a crack on a chain to expose a rheumy-eyed face topped with thin grey hair.

'Hello Doc,' she said. 'Remember me?'

'Who?' croaked the man through a mouthful of brown teeth. 'Who's there?'

'Sadie Ross. Eddie's wife.'

'Eddie Ross. It's been a long time.'

'He's not here Doc. He's away. But I've got someone.'

'I don't do that anymore.'

'Five thousand quid in Euros Doc, says you do.'

'No Sadie,' and he went to close the door, but her Doc Marten was in the gap.

'Yes you fucking do. I've got a friend that needs you.'

'Newham Hospital's not far.'

'Fuck off Doc, you know I wouldn't be here if I could take her to a hospital.'

'Her?'

'A mate. Family. Ten thousand.'

He thought for a moment, then said. 'I suppose you'd better come in. You can take your foot out of the door now, I need to release the chain.'

'No tricks,' said Sadie.

He gave her an old fashioned look, pushed the door to, released the chain, then opened it wide. 'Bullet I suppose,' he said.

Sadie nodded.

'Where is she?' he asked

'In that truck over there. She's out cold.'

Just as she said it, Kate arrived at her side. 'She's awake,' she said. 'But she's hurting.'

'Can she walk?' asked the doctor.

'I reckon.'

'How many of you are there?'

'Just three.'

'There's a loading bay for the shop at the back. You can get your vehicle through. I've got a back door, but she'll have to climb the stairs.'

'We'll make it,' said Sadie. 'And thanks Doc.'

'Don't thank me yet. And bring the money, I like to get paid in advance.'

Kate ran back to the truck as Sadie followed the doctor up a steep flight of stairs, through a kitchen that looked like it hadn't seen a mop and bucket for a year, and he shoved open a half glass door that looked over the Iceland car park at the back. There were some vans and motors parked up, but no sign of life. A steep flight of rusty steps led down to the ground. 'I hope your surgery is cleaner than your kitchen,' said Sadie.

'Take it or leave it.'

Just then the truck came through an arch and Kate drove it close to the steps. Sadie ran down and helped Poppy out of the passenger door. She groaned in pain, and between them Sadie and Kate helped her up the stairs. 'Get some dough for him Kate,' said Sadie when they were inside. 'And mind the truck. The last thing we need is for it to be nicked.'

'That would be unfortunate,' said Kate as she went back out again. 'I'll just be a minute.'

She came back with a pile of notes. 'How much is this in real money?' she asked.

Sadie took the money and said, 'Christ knows. But I reckon the Doc'll be happy. Now get back down. I'll be with you as soon as he's had a look at her.'

The doctor had led Poppy deeper into the flat and Sadie found her lying on a grubby sheet on an old hospital bed in an otherwise empty room. The doctor had pulled off her T-shirt and was examining the wound. 'You're a lucky girl,' he said. 'Not much internal damage from what I can see. I'll clean out the wound, bandage you up, give you some antibiotics, then you can go.'

'Will it hurt?' asked Poppy.

'Oh yes,' he replied. 'It'll hurt all right. Have some of this.' And he handed her a half-full bottle of brandy.

And it did. But Poppy was stoic although her face was the colour of the sheet she was lying on. Grey and sweaty. But the doctor was as gentle as he could be and Sadie held her hand throughout, and afterwards there were deep cuts from Poppy's nails on her palm.

Within an hour Poppy was bandaged and, although she stumbled as she got off the bed, she managed to walk back down the stairs with only Sadie's assistance. They left the doctor counting the Euros with a smile on his face. The first they'd seen since they arrived.

Once inside the truck, Kate drove again, and said. 'What do we do now?'

'Find somewhere safe to lie low, let Poppy get some rest, and we need to get rid of this truck and get another motor.'

'If Niki was here she'd steal one,' said Kate.

'But she's not,' said Poppy, her voice faltering.

'I'm so sorry, Poppy,' said Kate, gently.

'We'll hire one,' said Sadie. 'I got myself a new driving licence too, just in case.'

'You're a genius,' said Kate.

'I like to think so. And then we've got to get this money sorted. We can't carry it around for the rest of our lives.'

'What are we going to do with it?' said Kate. 'Christ, I never thought of that.'

'I did,' said Sadie. 'I opened a bank account in my new name.'

'You thought of everything,' said Kate.

'I had a good teacher in Eddie. Now just drive Kate. Let's get out of London and find a car-hire firm. Stanstead should do. Then we'll head north and dump this bloody truck somewhere.'

And that's exactly what happened.

* * *

Three weeks later three women boarded an early morning Eurostar to Paris. Two travelled together. An attractive dark-haired white woman in her mid-thirties with a fashionably short haircut, and a smaller, coffee coloured girl who walked with the aid of a stick, travelled first class. Down in second was another dark-haired girl in her twenties who was in the early stages of pregnancy. All paid for their tickets in cash, were expensively dressed, and carried only hand luggage. Once in Paris they took two taxis to the Eiffel Tower where they greeted each other like old friends, before taking another cab to the Charles De Gaulle airport where they purchased three first-class one-way tickets to New York, also with cash, and when they arrived they hired a limo and vanished into the metropolis.

At no time during their journey did anyone pay them any more attention than would normally be given to three beautiful women.

52

The beaches are wide and white in Ipanema, where the tall and tanned girl went walking; lined with hotels for tourists and longer staying visitors. Poppy, Sadie and Kate lay on sun loungers under brightly coloured umbrellas sipping pre-lunch drinks and watched the world go by. Poppy and Sadie on cocktails, Kate on straight orange juice. Poppy wore a black, one-piece bathing suit to hide the scars from Connie's bullet, Sadie wore a tiny bikini, and Kate wore a bikini too. But a slightly larger one, and over it a sarong to protect her swelling belly.

'Look at the arse on that,' said Sadie as a waiter in white shorts and T-shirt took drinks to a neighbouring table. 'I could eat my breakfast off it.'

'Don't you ever think of anything else?' said Kate lifting her sunglasses off her eyes and checking out his behind.

'You'd be surprised,' said Sadie. 'What I think about.'

'No I wouldn't,' said Kate. 'Do you think they're still looking? The men I mean.'

'Count on it. We fucked them up, killed a couple of them and nicked their dough. Left them to rot. Course they're still looking.'

'Do you think we killed the wrong ones?' asked Kate.

'Who knows? Maybe we should've killed them all, let God sort them out.'

'No. I liked the way we left Ali and Robbo together. Bastards.'

'Good result though,' said Sadie with a smile. 'I looked on the net. All hell broke loose at home.'

'Not a good result for Niki,' said Poppy.

'Sorry, darling,' said Sadie. 'You know I didn't mean it to sound like that.'

'I know,' said Poppy. 'Only I miss her so much.'

'We all do,' said Kate. 'We were family.'

'Still are,' said Sadie.

'Forever,' said Kate. 'And when baby comes, it's Nicholas if it's a boy, Nikita, if it's a girl.'

Under her shades, a tear rolled down from Poppy's eye.

'Don't cry girl,' said Sadie, touching her hand. 'We're here for you. Always.'

Poppy nodded, but the tears kept coming.

'You lot still carrying?' asked Kate, changing the subject.

'Not many,' Sadie lifted the handbag by her side and hefted it in her hand. 'Nine mill. You? Apart from junior, I mean.'

'I sleep with a 45 under my pillow.'

'Handy. Me, I find it's a bit of a passion-killer when a man finds a gun in bed.'

'Is that a pistol in your knickers or are you pleased to see me...'

Sadie laughed. 'You got that right. What about you, Poppy?'

'I've had enough of guns,' she replied, sadly.

'Course you have.'

'What would you do if Eddie or Robbo, or Ali came down those steps there?' Kate pointed at the flight leading to the bar of the hotel. 'Right this minute.'

'Shoot the fucker, leave everything and head for the airport. I've got my passport, or at least Susie Armstrong's, whoever she is, in my bag, cash, traveller's cheques and a packet of three. What else does a girl need?'

'Not much I've discovered. Poppy and I would be right behind you.'

'That's my girls. But they're not going to. Or at least I hope not. I'm looking forward to lunch and a siesta with the cabana boy.'

'I don't believe you,' said Kate.

'Nor did Eddie. But he believes me now. Another one of these, girls?' She tapped her glass with a long fingernail.

'Why not?'

'Yeah, why not?'